Time of Death

by

B. J. SANDIFORD

A DS Laura Hollis Novella

Inspired by the 1945 film 'Mildred Pierce'

Published by City Fiction

Copyright © 2019 B. J. Sandiford

This is a work of fiction. Names, characters, businesses, places,
events and incidents are either the products of the author's
imagination or used in a fictitious manner. Any resemblance to
actual persons, living or dead, or actual events is purely
coincidental.

ISBN: 978-1-910040-32-4

TIME OF DEATH

The blade, large, sharp and ugly had dried blood on its edges. All the man had to do was to press deeply and draw the knife from left to right and Detective Constable Hudson would be decapitated, just like the other two victims. Moonlight glinted off another thinner blade as the second assailant sliced the buttons from the detective's suit jacket.

Detective Sergeant Laura Hollis sat in a grey van with blacked-out windows opposite Hudson, beads of sweat were covering her face. Speaking into a microphone she said, "Wilkins and Collins, move in." The command was aimed at the two plain clothed police loitering in the shadows, smoking cigarettes.

Hollis observed the two men crouched beside Hudson. The pair wearing suits, were indistinguishable from any other businessman who worked in the area. It was only the knives they held that gave a clue to the fact that their work was not conducted behind a desk. The plain clothed officers were not going to reach Hudson in time. Laura Hollis looked at the knives and switched her gaze back to the distance the officers had to cover. The officers needed to run if they were to save Hudson. It was the one thing that the two officers could not do. Should she jump out of the van and assist Hudson? What if her sudden movement made the assailants either attack Hudson or run off? Weeks of painstaking planning would be ruined, or her colleague would be dead. Which was the best option to choose?

A tall lean man walked along the pavement towards the small group. He was yet another suit wearing man, intent on reading a text on his phone, rather than watching where he was stepping. He appeared to be oblivious of the three men crouched together on the ground. As he moved forward, he tripped over the assailant holding the knife to Hudson's throat. The phone fell to the ground. In the act of bending to pick it up, the man hit the assailant's wrist. The knife was dropped. The man kicked it away.

The drunkard, Hudson sprang into action at the same moment. He kicked his other assailant in the groin. The man groaned, dropped his knife and clutched his groin. Both attackers reeled from the unexpected violence. Detective Sergeant Lee Hudson aimed a punch at the solar plexus of the man who had sliced off his buttons. Hudson's saviour, Detective Chief Inspector Chappell hauled the other knife man to his feet and placed cuffs on him.

The plain clothed officers grabbed the recipient of Hudson's vicious punch and held his arms behind his back as Detective Sergeant Laura Hollis handcuffed him. She had sprinted from the van the moment Chief Inspector Chappell had appeared. Never had she been so happy to see him. Both assailants were escorted to a waiting police vehicle by the plain clothed officers, as Chappell, Hollis and Hudson walked over to the van.

Hollis turned to Chappell, "Where did you come from, sir? I didn't think that you were going to be here. You said that you were going to leave it up to me."

Chappell gave a wry smile, "And I did. I was however, in the area. I thought I'd help out. I did say I'd be watching." The Detective Inspector noticed Laura's flushed expression and the slight tightening of her lips. "Laura, I am not raining on your parade. You set this up. This was your operation. Well done. It was a success. You deserve all the credit for going out on a limb and making it work. Hudson, you equally deserve the credit for being prepared to act as a would-be victim."

"Thank you, sir. Thank you." Hudson appreciated the praise from his senior officer. He nodded and smiled at Chappell.

Chappell spoke to the rest of the team through their earpieces by using a microphone attached to the van's dashboard. The officers heard the congratulatory voice of their boss, "Well done everyone. A job well done. Process them and rest up in the office. Well done, commendations all round. You've stuck with this one. Hudson almost took one for the team. Good work, I'm proud of you all."

Chappell exited the van and sauntered away. Hollis' brown eyes bore resentfully into the back of his retreating head. She repeated her question, this time to Hudson.

"What was he doing here?" She needed an answer. "This was my operation. I handled it."

Hudson shrugged, "Forgive me Hollis, if I say I was pretty glad he was around. Anyway, you know what he's like. Our Detective Chief Inspector Chappell likes to be in at the kill. You didn't expect him to stay away did you? Just remember he trusted you, he let you run this operation. You're new to this team, this was your first test. I'd say you passed it."

The ringing of the telephone broke Detective Chief Inspector Mike Chappell's concentration. He had been intent on writing up a report.

"Chappell."

"Chief Inspector, it's Officer Barnes. There's a man here... he says..." Officer Barnes' voice trailed off.

"Yes, what did he say?" Chappell became alert, "come on, what do you want to tell me?"

"Sir, he says that he was out jogging this morning and, well, he found the body of a woman. He's come in to report it. He says that she is floating in a lake on his land."

"Thank you Officer Barnes. I'll deal with it." Chappell replaced the receiver, sipped at the cold coffee that had sat for some time on his desk and grimaced. He sighed deeply as he got to his feet and stepped out of his office into the large team room.

"Everyone, I need your attention."

"A drowning has been reported. We need to investigate the circumstances."

Detective Dave Sampson spoke up, "But we've only just finished..."

"Yes, and now you are back on duty," Chappell said. "I'm going to the scene. I'll expect you all back here within the hour."

Tarn Lake was a neat rectangle. It was part of an old quarry that had since filled with water and wildlife. With the sun shining and no breeze to ripple the water the lake resembled a mirror. The branches of a weeping willow hung low almost kissing the water. A family of ducks had settled on a bank watching the activity happening opposite them.

When Chappell reached the lake, the body of a woman; Jennifer Lindsay, had already been pulled from the water. The man who reported the drowning, Frederick Southpool, had been able to supply the name and details of the dead woman. Southpool had recognised her as one of the employees in his computing firm.

Jennifer lay on her back. Her hair had been pushed away from her pale face. Her eyes were closed, and her skin had developed a green tinge. Her clothes were sodden and covered in mud and weeds.

In the midst of the activity on the bank, Hazel Wilks crouched beside the body, the frame of her glasses glinted in the bright sunlight.

"Mike, there is bruising around the throat, and the eyes show petechiae; evidence of strangulation. There is a large dent, actually a hole on the back of the skull. It is doubtful that she fell into the water accidently. I do not think that this is the primary crime scene."

The coroner stood up, pulling off her rubber gloves. Chappell nodded, resisting the temptation to ask for further information. It would not be supplied if he asked.

The **coroner walked** away, indicating to a nearby white suited officer that the body be taken to one of the nearby ambulances.

"Mike." Hazel called out, "One thing you might need to know right now, is that this woman has a black eye."

"Oh?"

"Yes, it was healing. You just need to know that she had a black eye for at least a week. I don't know if it gives you a start but, there you go." She shrugged and got into a waiting car.

Chappell walked to where the body had been found. The lake was on private land, but it was beside a local footpath. Even though there were several 'No Trespass' signs on posts beside the path, there were any number of people who regularly broke down the wire fences and had picnics or sunbathed on the grass bank.

It would appear that the dead woman had also been having a meal beside the lake. He looked down at the remains of the picnic. There were two empty bottles of wine, packets of sandwiches, small pies and sausage rolls. One fact that struck him immediately was the absence of any drinking glasses. He would be interested in the forensic evidence from the bottles. Had the young woman, Jennifer Lindsay, and her companion each drunk from their own bottle?

Chappell bent down and put a hand on the grass. Just as he suspected, the grass was damp. It was not the weather for an al fresco meal, so where was the ground covering? His initial impression of the scene was that it was staged. Where was the sharp instrument that caused the hole in her skull? There was no blood on the ground or on the bank. Where had the body come from, more importantly who had brought the woman to the lake? He looked up and viewed the large but narrow and deep expanse of water. Another set of warning signs explained the fact to trespassers foolhardy enough to want to go for a swim.

He stood up and looked at the trees and grasses bordering the lake on all sides. At the far end of the lake was a car park which belonged to a local pub. There were a few cars present in it. He made a note to have the grounds around the pub looked at by the forensic team. Heading back to his own car, Mike had the distinct feeling that he was being watched. He scanned the lake and its surroundings once more. Chappell's car was the only one left on the grass bank. He looked at the trees, bushes and grasses on either side of his position. Everything was still. He stared at a clump of long grass and trees to his left. The feeling that he was being observed intensified. A movement caught his eye. A duck waddled out of the grass, into the water and set sail. Chappell breathed a sigh of relief. Just a duck. He had been so sure it was a person that had been watching him.

"Come."

Chappell put down the file he was reading and stared expectantly at his office door. His office was a neat square beige room with one window. He was fastidious about the organisation of his working space. The only personal memento in the room was the large framed photograph hanging on a wall. It showed Mike and two friends climbing the Matterhorn.

When it became clear that the person on the other side of the door was not going to respond to the single barked command, Chappell stood, rounded his desk and glanced at the picture. Just looking at the image brought back a rush of exhilaration and a jolt of adrenaline. He grinned to himself. Adrenaline and caffeine were two things he craved. Chappell was at the door in three long strides and opened it.

"Ah, you asked to see me Detective Chief Inspector?"

"Yes, I did. Come in Officer Barnes, Toby isn't it? Come in, sit down."

Officer Barnes walked in, swallowed visibly and sat down in one of the two visitor chairs Chappell indicated. "Did I do something wrong, sir? I mean I don't think..."

Chappell softened his normally severe expression. "No, not at all Officer Barnes. I just want to know about your impression of Mr Southpool. You were the first person he spoke to when he came to make his report. What was he like? What was his demeanour? "

"Well, it's funny you should ask."

"Why?"

"He was calm, very cold and controlled. I thought him to be..." Toby Barnes paused and then said "I can't think of the words. He was wrong. Something about him was wrong. Not normal." Barnes gesticulated randomly with his hands and shook his head.

"Chief Inspector, Mr Southpool did not panic. He seemed like he had all the time in the world. That struck me as not being right."

Chappell nodded and attempted to put the officer at his ease, "Let's look at it a different way. Describe the people you saw yesterday."

"Well, I came on duty at three in the afternoon. A few people were waiting, there were two tourists from America who thought they'd lost a passport. They were panicking. They hadn't, it was in the bottom of a bag of shopping. Then, there was someone who came in to report a car accident, a few other people wanted directions, and someone wanted to collect a form for something and then there was him, Southpool. I mean he came in, sat down and waited patiently to speak to me. He must have sat there for at least forty minutes, then he drops this bombshell. I mean, he hadn't made a fuss or pushed into the queue. He just waited patiently and announced that he'd found a dead body. Who does that?"

Chappell nodded thoughtfully. "Why did he come here?"

"He said that he'd been jogging when he saw the woman in the water. So, he ran back to his house, collected his car and drove over here. Why didn't he just ring the police? Just too controlled. If you ask me I think …"

Chappell stood up and said, "Thank you Officer Barnes you have been very helpful. I mustn't keep you." Chappell walked over to the door and held it open.

Chappell spoke to his team, "So to recap, we have the body of a woman found floating in a lake. The owner of the lake, Mr Frederick Southpool drives over here to inform us. As of yet we have no suspects." He looked around the incident room, noting the expressions of his assembled team. Preliminary investigations into the suspicious death of Jennifer Lindsay had begun.

Detective Sergeant Laura Hollis said, "Sir, do we really need to do this? We have a suspect; we know where to find him. Why drive over twenty minutes to a police station when you could just pick up a phone and ring? He's practically given us a confession."

Chappell raised the coffee cup he had been holding to his mouth, thought better of it and put the cup down on a table.

He replied, in a calm conversational tone, "Hollis, I am not aware that he confessed to anything. Mr

Southpool is a civic minded man who came to the police station to report the death of a woman on his land. That's a report, not a confession. As to what he reported, let's have a look. What exactly did he say?"

Hollis' pale brown cheeks burned with embarrassment. The eyes of her colleagues were upon her. She knew that she needed to just shut up and listen but sometimes she spoke first and thought later.

Chappell had turned to a white noticeboard already covered by photographs of the drowning incident and photocopies of Mr Southpool's report. He summed up the situation, "Yesterday, Frederick Southpool reported the death of Jennifer Lindsay. The coroner, from her observation at the scene, tells me that death by drowning is highly unlikely, but she had yet to carry out the formal autopsy. Jennifer Lindsay's eyes showed evidence of strangulation. Why is Mr Southpool saying that he knows nothing about how this young woman ended up in the lake on his land? Did he strangle her? What was this young woman doing by the lake anyway? I want answers to these questions. I want to know if she was murdered and if so, who ended her life?"

The team turned back to their computers and began sifting through the information they had already found. Jennifer Lindsay was a twenty-four year old female. Southpool had been able to provide information about her address and place of work. Jennifer worked for Southpool Computing and lived in a shared house on the edge of Bristol. Her body had been found in Tarn Lake which was near the village of Forge Tarn.

The result of questioning the villagers had revealed that although Jennifer Lindsay did not live in the area she was known to spend a lot of time in the village pub. Southpool had told the police that he had given Jennifer permission to visit the lake whenever she wished. Her presence by the lake had not surprised him although her death had. No-one in the village could swear to the fact that they had seen Jennifer in the area over the last few days. She had not visited the pub, nor any of the local shops.

Chappell walked over to Hollis' desk, picked up and read the research she had so far collected. He said, "I want you to have look at that lake, see if you can spot anything that may have been missed."

When Hollis did not immediately speak, he looked at her expectantly, raising his eyebrows.

Hollis uttered, "What, me? On my own?"

Chappell nodded, "Yes. I don't think it needs two people. Besides which, I'd like your impression of the place."

"Well, I …"

Chappell carried on, not allowing Hollis to speak, "You are pretty astute at picking up on atmosphere and identifying things that are out of place."

Hollis' response was one of genuine surprise, "You really think so?"

"Yes, yes I do. Besides you need to get more involved in the investigations. You've been here three months and you've only helped to plan one operation. It's time to see what you can do with this one.

"When you get back, I want both of us to visit the place where Jennifer Lindsay lived. We also need to visit Mr Southpool at his home."

Detective Constable Dave Sampson who was seated nearby interrupted Chappell, "Sorry to but in, but Mr Southpool is staying in the hotel down the road. He said that he had a few business meetings in town, and he didn't feel comfortable living in his house at this time. I've got his details here." Sampson proffered a sheet of paper which was covered in his distinctive scrawl.

"Thanks, Dave."

Chappell walked away. As soon as he was out of earshot, Sampson said, "No pressure Hollis. No pressure." He grinned at her, winked and returned his attention to his work.

Hollis gave him a tight smile, hung her head and allowed her long golden brown curly hair to hide her face. No pressure indeed. Chappell had asked her to take a hand in the last operation. No doubt this was another one of Chappell's tests. She reached out for her bottle of water and took a swig.

The surface of Tarn Lake reflected the overcast sky above it. Police warning tape billowed in the wind. Yellow incident signs had been placed by the area where the body had been found in the water and were dotted along the footpath. The cold breeze rippled the surface and ruffled her hair. Hollis shivered, whether it because of the temperature or because she was standing in a desolate crime scene she could not tell. She pulled her suit jacket around her slim frame and crossed her arms.

Hollis had studied the crime scene photos before arriving at the lake. The body had been found by one of the short sides of the lake. At the other end there was the car park behind the local pub. If she could see the pub and the few cars parked beside it, then the opposite was true. How was the body placed in the lake without the assailant being seen?

Could it have been done by using a boat? Hollis began to walk around the perimeter of the lake. From the photos she had seen a clump of bushes beside a tree. She headed towards it. Hollis missed it at first, but she stubbed her toe on a rusted mossy pole lying flat in the grass. She knelt to look at it. Connected to it was a chain that was fastened on its other end to an old rowing boat. It lay low in the water, weeds and slime were in the bottom. She inspected it and then looked at the chain that fastened it to the bank. "Why use a new chain to connect a rotting boat to the bank? This boat doesn't look like it is worth keeping." Hollis had a habit of speaking to herself. It allowed her to marshal her thoughts.

She looked at the boat again, picked up a long twig that lay on the ground and dipped it into the slime that coated the inside of the bottom of the boat. The twig went through the boat into the water beneath it. She looked around the area beside the boat. In the mud near the water's edge was a set of footprints and some ash from a cigarette. The ash looked fresh. She bent down to take photographs and took a sample of the ash. Standing up, she looked towards where her car was parked. If someone had stood in this position, they would have had a clear view of what the police had been doing when Jennifer Lindsay's body had been recovered. Had that person been the killer?

The drive back to the police station allowed Hollis to shape her ideas about the possible murder of Jennifer Lindsay. The fact that bothered her the most was the picnic. The way the picnic was laid out did not seem like a realistic thing to do. Was someone pointing the police in a particular direction? Why? The attacker would have been better served by not leaving any clues whatsoever. "Why?" She spoke the question out loud.

Hollis met with Chappell as soon as she returned to the station. She told him of her uneasiness of the staged picnic.

Chappell said, "You have that feeling too? I sensed it when I was there. I wanted to know if you would pick up on it. I'm glad it wasn't just me."

Hollis smiled. "It was obvious if you think about it."

Chappell tilted his head, regarded her for a few seconds and asked, "If it was that obvious, why did the killer do it?"

Hollis opened and then closed her mouth. She shrugged, unhappy that she did not know the answer.

Chappell said, "When we know the answer to that, we will know the answer to everything. I think that the picnic is the key to us solving this murder."

Hollis had been the first to return to the incident room and the rest soon gathered bearing further information. Chappell sensed their nervous energy. His team were alert and had information. As always, he had ordered coffee and pastries from the canteen to be delivered. Once they had eaten, Chappell asked for the results of their research.

"Sampson you start."

Dave Sampson said, "Jennifer Lindsay, as we know is, or rather was, female, Caucasian and twenty-four years old. She was a computer whizz kid with a glittering future in front of her. She lived in a shared house with people she knew from school who were now studying at Bristol University or had just graduated. I interviewed her fellow housemates." He paused to look down at his notes, "none of the housemates had a bad thing to say about her. She kept herself to herself and mainly kept to her room. They said that you would never know if she was in unless you knocked on her door. I had a look at her room, it was tidy and clean. Everything was well ordered. Her pride and joy was her computing equipment. I've had that brought in so that it can be looked at. On the surface though she does not look like she has anything to hide.

"Everyone in the house knows each other from school or study but it appears that they have separate social lives."

Chappell nodding, looked around at the rest of the team and asked, "Does anyone have anything else to add?"

"Yes sir," Detective Sergeant Lee Hudson answered. "I've been trying to track down her social life. She didn't have much of one. She used to frequent the Mountlee Pub near Frederick Southpool's house, not recently though. We took a photo of Jennifer Lindsay from her room and took it to the village with us. The staff at the pub recognised her picture and said that she used to be in there at different times of the day. Sometimes on her own and sometimes with different people. Her companions seemed quite young; all they did was just have a few drinks and chat. She did not argue with any of them."

Chappell nodded. "Why the pub there? She lives in Bristol and the business is in Bristol. What would she be doing drinking close to her employer's home? There is still a lot we need to find out. One thing I am certain of is that Jennifer Lindsay did not accidentally drown. That's my personal opinion for now, we'll see when the pathology report comes in."

Chappell asked Sampson to set up meetings with the housemates. "I also think that we need to investigate the background of Mr Southpool a little more." He said. "That man interests me; I'm suspicious and surprised that he drove over here to report the death instead of using the nearest phone. That one fact in itself, stands out."

Jennifer Lindsay's lodgings were much as Chappell suspected the house would be. It was a red brick terraced house that had seen generations of tenants passing through its rooms. There was nothing to distinguish it from any house along that street. From the outside the house was clean and tidy. Hollis stood across the road from the house and took a few moments to look at the house. There were no twitching curtains or ghostly shadows hiding behind the windows. Crossing over the road, she joined Chappell as he knocked on the front door. After a few minutes the door was opened by a young expensively dressed woman clothed entirely in black.

The woman asked, "Yes, may I help you?"

Chappell's attention was caught by the pile of packing crates he saw in the hall behind her.

He asked, "Is someone moving out or in?"

A smile played around the woman's mouth, "My, my aren't you observant? You must be a policeman. I'm Elle Latimer." She held out a hand, "You are?"

Chappell looked directly at Elle, did not take her hand and said, "Sorry, I'm Detective Chief Inspector Chappell and this is Detective Sergeant Hollis. May we come in?"

"Certainly. I've been expecting you." Elle stood aside to let Chappell and Hollis enter. "I'm glad you were prompt; I have to go out soon."

Hollis who was slightly taller than average height for a woman at five feet and seven inches towered over the diminutive Elle Latimer.

The interior of the house matched the outside. It was equally well kept. As Hollis and Chappell walked deeper into the hallway, they had to navigate past even more boxes and crates. Elle led the way to a large communal lounge and sat down on a red velvet sofa. Chappell sat down on a chair opposite her while Hollis walked over to the picture window that dominated the far wall. As she did so she made a cursory inspection of the room.

"Now tell me, Detective Chief Inspector Chappell what is it that we can help you with? The other policeman came and told us about what had happened to poor Jennifer. I thought that it was an accident?"

"That is what we are investigating Ms Latimer."

"Is that so?" Elle Latimer looked Chappell directly in the eyes and smiled. Chappell did not return the smile. Instead, he narrowed his eyes and followed Hollis' movements around the room. He let a few seconds elapse before he spoke.

"Ms Latimer..", he said.

"Elle. Please do call me Elle."

Chappell cleared his throat, "Ms Latimer, please can you give us some background information about Jennifer Lindsay?"

Elle smiled and asked, "Background information such as what?"

Chappell did not smile back. He asked, "Were you friends? Did you socialise with each other? Do you know who her friends were?"

Elle still smiling said, "I see. In short, no. Jennifer and I had very little in common other than the fact that we shared a house and some mutual friends. Jennifer just wasn't my kind of person." Elle shrugged her thin shoulders and crossed her arms.

Chappell asked, "Who were your mutual friends? Is there anything you can tell us about her other friends?"

Elle said, "Everyone in this house. We either met at university or we knew of each other through people that we knew. Jennifer was a...Jennifer was gay. I'm not, so I really didn't associate too much with that circle of people. When she was at home she was quiet, but she wasn't at home that often. She spent a fair amount of time with her girlfriend, I seem to recall."

Chappell asked, "Can you tell us the name of Jennifer's girlfriend?"

Elle shook her head. "No. I didn't take the time to find out. I wasn't interested in Jennifer; who she saw or what she did. Peter or Jack might be able to help you."

"Do you know if she was at home over the last few days. We need to build up a picture of her last movements."

Elle frowned, thought about the question and then shook her head once again. She stared at Chappell, opened her mouth, closed it, then said, "Chief Inspector Chappell. That is such a mouthful. Don't you have something else I can call you by?"

"Chief Inspector is just fine. You were about to say?"

Elle pouted and replied, "I'm an architect and I've been working some long hours to finish a project. I've been travelling for the past few days. I only got back on Thursday, no sorry, Friday." She blushed and began to pluck at a loose thread on a nearby cushion. "The first I knew about anything was when the other policeman knocked on the door. I did not see Jennifer when I came back on Friday and I have not seen her since."

Elle stared at her feet, "Look, I wasn't keen on Jennifer, but I am sorry that she's dead." She stopped plucking at the cushion and held her hands in her lap.

Chappell asked, "Is there anyone she was particularly close to in this house?"

"She was close to Jack and Peter. Mind you she had a fight with Jack. Those boxes in the hall belong to him."

Chappell asked, "When you say fight, what was it about? Was it physical?"

Elle thought for a moment and said, "I'm not sure what it was about, but I did see Jennifer slap Jack and he punched her in return. He gave her a black eye. Jack is normally a gentle giant but, I've got to say, I think that she probably deserved it. She split up from her girlfriend recently and she had been totally unbearable to live with. Like I said, I barely had anything to do with her, but people were complaining about her all the time."

"Where can we find Jack? What's his surname?"

"Jack Danvers. He's in the process of moving out. Those are his boxes in the hall. I think his new address is on the board in the hallway too."

Chappell narrowed his eyes as he looked at Elle and asked "Elle, does Jack's moving out have anything to do with this fight with Jennifer? Was there anything else behind his moving out?"

"Possibly. I don't know for sure. I do know that Jennifer had really pissed him off about something and he had said that enough was enough. To be honest though, I suspect he probably just wanted to move closer to the hospital."

Chappell queried, "The hospital?"

Elle said, "Yes, Jack is a junior doctor. He works incredibly long hours and comes back at all hours of the day and night."

"So, at this stage is there nothing else you could tell us about Jennifer?"

Elle gave Chappell a flirtatious smile and said, "No, but if you give me your card I'll ring you if I remember anything."

Chappell attempted to look apologetic and lied, "I'm sorry I don't have any cards, but Detective Sergeant Hollis will give you one of hers. Please do not hesitate to ring if you remember anything. It could be important. We'll be upstairs looking at Ms Lindsay's room."

Chappell turned and headed for the stairs located to one side of the hallway. Hollis walked back from her position at the end of the room and handed a card to Elle Latimer. Elle took the card but did not take her eyes away from looking at Chappell.

Jennifer's room was exactly as it had been described. It was immaculate. The room was painted the same off-white as the rest of the rooms they had seen. The only colour in the room came from the turquoise duvet cover and bright green pillows. There were no clothes draped over chairs or on the bed; all were folded on shelves or hanging up in the wardrobe or on hooks on the back of the door.

Chappell and Hollis searched methodically looking

for anything that would provide a clue to her character and why she had been killed.

Hollis muttered softly to herself.

Chappell looked over at her, "Did you say something?"

"Yes," she replied. "I just wanted to know who Jennifer was."

Chappell looked around him, "That's what we are here to find out."

A door closed softly. Chappell heard footsteps walking along the pavement.

Hollis pointed to the collection of make-up organised in a number of small decorative baskets. "Jennifer Lindsay used a fair amount of make-up. Some of that stuff is really expensive. I should know, I use some of the same products. She took care of herself." Hollis carried on with her search.

There was a cork board on one wall, it was covered with receipts, tickets to gigs, concerts and a few shows, some of them bore dates for the coming few months. On the front of the wardrobe was a collage of photographs.

Hollis studied some of them and shouted "Bingo."

Chappell was startled by Hollis' shout. "What, what was that?"

"Jennifer Lindsay's girlfriend. Look at these." She pointed to the photographs; Jennifer had her arms around the same woman in a few of them. In others the same woman had her arms around Jennifer and in the last few Jennifer and the mystery woman were kissing. The pictures showed Jennifer Lindsay in happier times. Her blonde hair was cut into an asymmetric bob, short on one side and long on the other. Jennifer was grinning at the camera as she waved a bottle of beer in front of her.

Chappell said, "I wonder how recent these are." He pulled the photos from the board turned them over and checked for date stamps. There weren't any. Chappell and Hollis searched through everything they could find; books, folders, drawers and the wardrobe looking for more photographs or anything else that could give them some idea of how Jennifer Lindsay had lived. There was no evidence of any hidden life or anything that she would not want anyone to see.

Chappell who was looking through a chest of drawers asked, "Hollis, what did you make of Ms Latimer?"

"She really did not care for Jennifer. Beyond that, I felt that she was hiding something."

"Why do you think that?" Chappell queried her as she crouched down to look under the bed.

"Elle Latimer said nothing to explain her movements over the last few days. I would have expected her to say what she had been doing."

"You expected her to volunteer the information? Some people don't Hollis. Remember you will need to be as objective as possible when you investigate. Do you think that you can do that?"

"Yes, certainly." She paused, "It's just that…" Hollis would have continued but a door slammed below. There was a heavy tread on the stairs. A face appeared at the open door of the bedroom.

"Who are you? What are you doing?" A young sandy haired, freckle faced man asked. His face and eyes were red as if he had been crying.

Chappell said, "I'm Detective Chief Inspector Chappell and this is Detective Sergeant Hollis. Who are you?"

"Oh, I see. Peter Riggs. I've come back to see you. I live here. Jennifer was my best friend. We went to school together. I can't.... can't..." Peter's face crumpled as he burst into tears.

Chappell reached out a hand and guided the boy to a chair. "No, I can't sit in here, let's go to my room." Chappell and Hollis followed him up a short flight of stairs to another landing. Peter opened the door of his room. The room was messy. There were piles of clothes and books on every surface. The small bin was overflowing with takeaway food containers. The room smelt of stale food and body odour. Chappell was tempted to open the window, but it had begun to rain, large raindrops were hammering against the glass.

Peter stopped sobbing long enough to say, "Sorry about the mess. Sit down." He pointed to two chairs, "I mean just shove some stuff on the floor and sit down."

Chappell and Hollis did as instructed while Peter sat on his bed. He wiped his eyes and runny nose on the arm of his grey sweatshirt. "Is there anything you can tell me? The policemen who came yesterday said it was an accidental drowning, but if you are here today that means that you are not sure, right?" Peter directed his question to Chappell.

Chappell replied, "We need to be sure."

Peter said, "She's dead and someone was with her. What do you need to be sure about?"

Chappell spoke with a calm patient tone, "Life is not always so clear cut. We need to know that we have come to the correct conclusion. To do that we need to gather as much evidence as possible. Her death may well have been accidental but then again it may not have been."

Peter hung his head; his sobbing subsided and instead became a series of hiccups. His shoulders rose and fell convulsively. "Is there anything I can help you with?"

"Yes, was Jennifer seeing anyone? Is there anyone in particular that she was dating?"

"Jennifer had been seeing Lisa Blaine." Peter paused, swallowed loudly and continued, "They broke up not that long ago."

Chappell said, "It was quite recent…"

Hollis interrupted Chappell and asked, "Do you know why?" It was not in her nature to be silent during an interview. Chappell turned his head sharply and looked at her.

Peter nodded and said, "Lisa cheated on her. It broke Jennifer's heart, it really did. She thought that Lisa was special, but Lisa didn't feel that way."

Hollis looked at Chappell. He waved his hand, motioning at her to continue with her questioning. She asked, "How long had they been together?"

"Three years, I think. It was definitely a while. Then Lisa started seeing someone else and didn't make a point of hiding her new relationship."

"What do you mean not hiding it?"

"Jennifer and I regularly went out for dinner. On this occasion we had gone to a local restaurant and there was Lisa with her new girlfriend. They were just leaving, holding hands and staring into each other's eyes. It was sickening."

Hollis asked, "What did Jennifer do?"

"She had a bit of a cry. Once she came to terms with what she'd seen she started looking for a new job. She said that there was no way that she was living in Bristol where she would be constantly bumping into Lisa and her new partner."

Chappell resumed his questioning, "Did she follow through with her plans?"

Peter nodded and replied, "Oh yes, she wrote out a new CV and applied for as many jobs as she could. She went to quite a few job interviews and collected quite a few offers for jobs. She was making up her mind when this happened. I know that she told her boss Frederick Whatshisname and he bit her head off."

Chappell's eyes narrowed. He watched Peter intently as he asked his next question, "Frederick Southpool. Do you have any idea what he said exactly?"

Peter's face began to crumple. He started crying. Chappell looked around the room while he waited for Peter to stop sobbing.

Eventually Peter said, "Jennifer said that he swore at her and called her all the names under the sun. She really hated that guy. She really liked Samuel though, he's the assistant."

Hollis asked, "What did she say about him?"

Peter sniffed, "She said that Samuel was the one who spoke sense in that business. Samuel really looked out for the employees while Southpool just thought the employees were robots. He expected them to work, never take holidays and hardly ever gave them pay rises. I think that she was working on some program for Southpool, something different to her normal job."

Chappell asked, "Do you know what it was?"

"No, he wanted her to work on it at his home. She borrowed Jack's motorbike to get there. Southpool lives way out in the back of beyond and Jennifer said that she needed to make sure she could get home. She certainly wasn't staying under his roof."

"When she said that, did you get the impression that there was something between them or that Mr Southpool wanted there to be?" asked Hollis.

Peter thought for a moment. "I don't think so." Peter spoke slowly, voicing his thoughts as they came to him. "Jennifer is...I mean was..." Peter stopped and sniffed loudly. Hollis handed him a tissue from one of her pockets. "Thank you." Peter blew his nose and blinked back his tears. "Attractive. Men and women were attracted to her. Her preference is...I mean was girls. I don't know what Mr Southpool was after, but Jennifer was only interested in the project. She could be single minded like that. She believed in this project and that was the only thing on her mind."

Chappell asked, "Was the project successful? Were they developing what Mr Southpool wanted?"

Peter shrugged and said, "No idea. I'm a Psychology graduate. All I need to know about a computer is that it works when I turn it on. Jennifer seemed happy about the progress they had been making."

Hollis asked, "Peter, we've been trying to account for Jennifer's movements over the past few days. Is there anything you can tell us about that?"

Peter replied, "I...er...no, not really." Peter paused and got up. He walked over to the window and looked out over the street. The rain had stopped. He opened the window and took a gulp of fresh air, "I've been pretty busy myself. I just assumed that she was around." Peter sniffed loudly.

Hollis asked "Was there any reason for Jennifer to

go to Forge Tarn Lake? Did she go on her own?"

Peter nodded, "Yes, she went all the time. She found it peaceful there."

Chappell asked, "How did she normally get there?"

"By bus, there are two buses you need to get there and then you have to walk. Some of us from the house and our other friends went with her a few times. It was such a trek that we would go to the pub and pay for a taxi to come back. We felt sorry for her after she split up with Lisa, so we kept her company." Peter smiled fondly at the memory. "Jennifer said that she got some of her best ideas for her work when sitting by the lake."

Chappell asked "Who is we? We've spoken to Ms Latimer and she really did not care for Jennifer and I understand that Jack Danvers and Jennifer had a fight."

Peter said "Me, Jack and a few other people who still live around here. A big contingent of us came down to Bristol and we meet up from time to time. Jennifer was in a pretty bad way after her break up, so we tried to check in on her when time allowed."

Hollis asked, "Peter, would Elle know who Jennifer's girlfriend was?"

"Of course! Lisa Blaine is Elle's boss. Elle knew exactly what was going on with Jennifer."

Chappell and Hollis looked at each other. Chappell shook his head at Hollis.

Chappell got up and smiled sympathetically at Peter. "We'll be off now. I'll give you my card. If you think of anything, no matter how small just ring me."

Hollis and Chappell nodded their thanks and made their way down the stairs. She took down the details of Jack Danvers' new address, while Chappell left the house and walked over to the police car. The engine was running by the time Hollis reached the car a few seconds later.

"Sir, Elle Latimer just lied to us."

"Yes, she did, didn't she? What would you do about that?"

"Well, I'd go back in there and ask her. Sir, I don't know why we aren't talking to her right now."

"Because she left soon after we started searching Jennifer's room."

"We can't let her get away with lying to the police."

Chappell smiled, "I think she'll keep Hollis. What did you make of Peter Riggs?"

"Peter's answer about not knowing if Jennifer was home over the weekend seemed vague. Come to think of it he was pretty vague about his own movements. I just wish we could get some idea of why she was killed."

"Hey, you there. I think you've overcharged me." The man waved his hotel bill under the manager's nose and glared at him.

"No sir, I do not think so."

"Read it, go on read it. That charge there for £500. What's that for? There's a mistake on this bill. I want you to fix it."

The manager smiled pleasantly at the outraged man. "Please let me have the receipt." He raised his hand to take the paper.

The customer dropped the receipt onto the counter and jabbed a finger into the manager's chest.

The manager did not react to the show of rudeness.

The customer said, "No-one and I mean no-one makes a fool out of me. So, you can take that charge you have just slipped on to my bill off."

The manager read the receipt carefully and looked at the hotel guest.

"Ah, yes, I see a mistake has been made. This hotel bill is for a Mr and Mrs Brown, whereas you sir, are Mr Henry Spires and the lady who has been keeping you company is Mrs Helen Ronson. Do you wish me to take further action with this payment? Who exactly is making this payment? Is it Mr Spires or Mr Brown? I see that this is a corporate card. I would have to ring and enquire how Mr and Mrs Brown happen to be using this card and staying at the hotel for a romantic break. Do you want me to investigate this issue further?"

The manager stared into Mr Spires's eyes and watching with detached interest as the guest's cheeks turned from a suffused red to bloodless white. Henry Spires began to tremble and looked about the hotel reception for an escape route.

Henry Spires said, "I...I...No, no that's fine. Take the payment."

The manager said, "Very good sir. I will process the bill as it stands. Have a very good day. Would you like the porter to carry your bags?"

"No, no that's ok." Henry Spires hurried away from the reception area.

If he had not been working, the manager would cheerfully have wrung Mr Henry Spires' neck. As it was, he retained his professional manner, smiled and waited to serve the next guest.

It did not take long to reach Jack Danvers' flat.

Hollis had called ahead. Danvers had said that he would be in. He had taken a few days off work in order to move and sort out his new flat. It was not hard to identify him, for he was carrying a packing crate from a rental van and heading towards the address that they had been given. Jack Danvers was a well-built man who stood well over six feet tall. It was unusual for Chappell to meet someone who was as tall as himself.

"Mr Danvers?" he asked.

"Yes, who are you?" Danvers stopped in his tracks and stared at Hollis and Chappell.

Hollis spoke up, "Detective Sergeant Hollis and this is Detective Chief Inspector Chappell. We're hoping that you can answer some questions about Jennifer Lindsay for us Mr Danvers."

"So, has that stupid bitch decided to press charges? Let me tell you, she hit me first. I just retaliated. Why doesn't she do everyone a favour and end everything like she keeps saying?"

Hollis blushed and Chappell coughed gently. He cleared his throat and spoke, "No Mr Danvers, Jennifer Lindsay is not pressing charges. She is dead. We understand that you had an altercation with her last week which resulted in you punching her. May we come in?"

Danvers paled, nodded, kicked open his front door and led the way to a lounge filled with boxes, piles of books, potted plants and hi-fi equipment.

"Sit down, if you can find a space."

Hollis sat on a leather stool while Chappell decided to stand. Danvers put his box down and looked thoughtfully at the police officers.

"So, she's dead. I know what I just said sounds

bad, but she really did provoke me."

Chappell nodded understandingly, "Why don't you explain."

"Jennifer was normally alright to get along with, but after she split up with Lisa, her girlfriend, she became really moody and unpredictable. I used to let her borrow my motorbike. I'm a doctor so I really need it to get about. If I wasn't using it, of course I would let her borrow it. Then she started behaving really strangely, she started going out at all hours of the day and night on my bike. She had an accident. Oh, she paid to get the damage fixed but at that point I said enough was enough. I told her that I did not want her using my bike again, she agreed. The next thing I know she is riding my bloody bike, without my permission and I have to go to work. I had to take public transport to the hospital and a taxi back home when I'd finished. When I did get back she wasn't even home, and my bike was nowhere to be seen.

"When she finally got back I shouted at her. She screamed back something about guys bothering her and taking advantage and slapped me round the face. I just lost it and punched her. After that I made sure that I took my keys off her and the next morning started looking for somewhere else to live."

Hollis asked, "Mr Danvers, what did she mean about being bothered?"

"Look, all I know is that once or twice she complained about guys trying to pick her up when she was out socialising.

Jack looked around the room taking care not to look at the police officers. He sighed, "What I just said about her earlier, I'm sorry. Normally, she was fine but after she found out about Lisa cheating on her she just became really erratic. Speak to her one minute she'd be fine, the next minute she'd bite your head off. It was like she deliberately wanted to start a fight with someone, anyone. She was just so unreasonable."

Jack wrapped his arms around himself and asked, "Have you spoken to Peter yet?" Jack did not wait for an answer, but continued, "He's turned into one creepy guy. That's another reason for me moving out. The atmosphere in that place was getting to me. Elle, Jennifer and Peter were just starting to annoy me. To be honest I had decided to leave long ago but I just needed to get my act together. But anyway, Jennifer and Peter went to school together, then the same university but different subjects and then they ended up sharing a house. Peter is...was in love with Jennifer. He adored her."

Hollis interrupted, "But she was seeing someone else?"

"Yes, she was. This thing with Lisa really shook her up and affected her. Peter tried to support her as best he could for a while. He was a good friend to her and then ... I don't know..." Jack shrugged and became lost in thought for a moment, "I don't know, maybe he realised that he did not stand a chance with Jennifer. He actively started to sabotage her."

Chappell frowned, "How do you mean?"

Jack said, "She'd ask him to do things for her, things he would have done before, but now he would say no or just not do them."

Chappell said, "I still don't understand."

"They used to do their shopping together or one would do it and the other would give the money for their bit. Now though, Peter wouldn't do her shopping. He'd say that he didn't have enough money, or he'd left his money behind at home. He would agree to pick her up from somewhere and not do it. He's got a small car and before he was happy to be her chauffeur. Now though, he wouldn't offer to give her a lift or anything. I remember a few weeks ago he was supposed to be meeting her by that lake in Forge Tarn. She had already headed out there and Peter told me that he couldn't be bothered to go. She used to go there all the time with her girlfriend. I think she was supposed to be meeting some new person there. Peter said that Jennifer would have to sort herself out. He said that he was fed up with acting like Jennifer's doormat and she could start wiping her feet on someone else.

"I mean, it was clear that Peter was in love with Jennifer and she never acknowledged him. He would go out of his way for her. When I needed my bike, he would go out of his way to collect her. Then his attitude changed. I guess if you have to listen to someone crying on your shoulder about how much they love someone else and how no one else will do, you will get fed up. I lived at the top of the house on the other side of Peter's room. There were times when Jennifer's door was open, and I would see Peter in Jennifer's room sitting on her bed or looking at her things."

Chappell asked, "Was Jennifer in the room?"

Jack shook his head, "No and that's what I mean by creepy. He was becoming a bit obsessive about her. I just thought it was high time I got out of there and after the fight with Jennifer and Peter's behaviour I just felt it was time to leave."

Chappell asked, "What were your movements over

the last few days?"

"Oh, I'm a suspect am I?" Jack chuckled dryly. "Sorry didn't mean to laugh. Well I've been moving in here. Loads of colleagues either helped me to build my furniture or drink my beer. I don't think I've been on my own until just before you arrived."

"One last question; did Elle and Jennifer get on?"

Jack waved his hands in an unsure manner and said, "They did to begin with but then some guy that Elle was dating or working with, I'm not sure, started taking more of an interest in Jennifer. Elle didn't like it. Jennifer could be a real live wire and she got on with everyone. Elle just objected to the fact that Jennifer started flirting with this guy. Jennifer could be a real flirt at times. It didn't go down well with Elle at all."

Chappell nodded and raised his eyebrows encouragingly at Jack, willing him to expand his answer.

Jack obliged, "I mean take the week just gone, Tuesday I think it was. One of Elle's colleagues was at the house asking for some drawings that Elle had left behind. He was still there being entertained by Jennifer by the time Elle got back later that evening."

Hollis asked, "Are you sure it was Tuesday?" She checked the notes she had made on Elle Latimer's interview.

Jack replied, "Yes definitely. I had started my packing and the guy was there, so I put him to work. Elle was fuming. I'm amazed they didn't come to blows but then maybe Jennifer had learnt that if you slap people they might hit you back."

Hollis asked, "Do you know his name?"

Jack nodded, "Yeah, Andy something. He was a

friendly enough guy. I just asked him to lift a few heavy things for me into the back of the van. Well, if that's all, I have to get on. I have to return the van this afternoon or I get charged a penalty fee."

Chappell turned to leave, "I hope you enjoy your new home Mr Danvers." He and Hollis left and made their way to the car.

"You drive Hollis, I need to think."

Chappell was silent throughout the drive. Hollis had parked in the car park of the police station when Chappell roused himself and said, "No, let's go to Southpool Computing. So far we are getting conflicting information. Elle knew who Jennifer's girlfriend was, Peter was obsessive and actively sabotaged Jennifer."

"Sir, do you think Jack was telling the truth?"

"It would appear so but I'm not taking anything at face value. Make sure you get the names of the people who helped Jack move into his flat. Right, let's go to Southpool Computing."

As Hollis drove Chappell said, "Hollis I want you to start asking more questions when we carry out interviews. Don't feel that you have to wait for me. You've been good, jumping in when paths need to be followed. I want you to do more of that."

Hollis nodded, "Yes sir, I will." She shifted in her seat, made a show of looking in her wing mirror and smiled.

Another victim, another complaint.

Miranda Holland screamed at the man, "You can't do that! I can't afford it. I don't have the money."

The blackmailer responded, "Would you rather I tell what I know?"

Miranda shook her head and said "No."

The man smiled at her and said in a calm conversational tone, "Then, you need to pay up. I'm not asking for much just £250, same as always."

Miranda wailed at him, "I can't keep paying you. I'm not made of money."

"Your husband is though." The man continued speaking in a pleasant tone, "Your husband clearly gives you a generous allowance. You just need to spend less on clothes, shoes and lovers."

Tears sprang to the woman's eyes, her hands trembled as she dug into her bag and produced a wad of notes.

Her blackmailer, threw his cigarette on the ground, viciously grinding it underfoot. Triumph glittered in his eyes as he took the cash. He took his time counting through the money slowly, rearranging some of the notes, so that the different denominations were together.

Miranda's voice was full of rage as she said, "It's all there."

Her blackmailer nodded and said, "Yes, it always is. I look forward to next month's payment."

"There won't be another payment." The woman thrust her face forward, that's the last payment you're getting from me. I don't know what I'll do but, I'm not paying you anymore. You've been warned."

The man chuckled, shoved the money into the back pocket of his jeans and walked away.

Southpool Computing was based in a business centre. The park was landscaped with well-kept green lawns and young saplings. All the office blocks were identical low glass fronted units. In the bright sunshine and blue sky, the buildings gave the appearance of mirrored cubes reflecting the grass and trees. Southpool Computing consisted of a set of these interconnected structures. A low sign set in the grass proclaimed the fact that you had reached Southpool Computing. Outside the main building the car park was filled with several expensive looking cars. It was full except for one space which was reserved for the Company President.

Chappell pointed to the empty space and said, "Since he's sitting in a hotel conducting his meetings, I think that you can park right there Hollis."

Hollis parked. Both police officers got out to walk the short distance to the entrance.

"You can't park there." A voice called out from an open window. It was hard to see through the window since it was mirrored.

"Police." Hollis called out. The window immediately closed.

The reception area had a large console where a receptionist and security guard sat. Behind them were two workmen who were taking down a 'Southpool Computing' sign. Dust floated down as it was moved causing the receptionist to cough. A door to the left of the reception opened and six people came in.

"End of an era", commented one person. Another said "Thank God! Hated the lying cheating bastard." Four of the people nodded at this last statement.

"What's going on here?" Chappell asked.

The second speaker answered, "The takeover, that's what's happening. The high and mighty Frederick Southpool gambled and lost. Who are you?"

"I'm Detective Chief Inspector Chappell and this

is Detective Sergeant Hollis. I'd like to speak to the person in charge. Who is that?"

"That would be me." A deep bass voice came from behind Chappell, as a squat dark haired man walked through a doorway on the other side of the reception. He approached Chappell holding out his hand. "I am the Vice-President of Southpool Computing. I am Samuel Adesinsi. How may I help you?" He smiled at Hollis and waited for the police officers to reply.

Chappell shook Samuel's hand. "Is there somewhere a little more private that we can go?"

"Of course, follow me." Samuel retraced his steps with the police officers following him and made his way to a functional looking grey cube of an office. There was a window in one wall that let in little light due to the tree planted right outside the building. Samuel sat behind the imitation wooden desk and indicated that Chappell and Hollis sit in the two visitors' chairs arranged on the other side of it.

Chappell looked appraisingly at Samuel. The man was in his forties, wearing a blue shirt, navy tie and navy trousers. He had intelligent large brown eyes and a quick smile.

Samuel gave the police officers a warm smile and asked, "How can I help you? Is this anything to do with the fact that Fred hasn't come into work today?"

Chappell nodded, "Yes, very much so. Can I ask you for your impression of Frederick Southpool?"

Samuel asked, "Why, is he in some sort of trouble?" Chappell noted Samuel's evasion.

Hollis spoke up, "If you could just answer the question please."

Samuel smiled. There was a vindictive curl to his

lips, he gave a short laugh which sounded more like a snort of disgust. "Frederick Southpool is probably the least likeable person you could ever hope to meet. He will offer you the world, anything to get you to do what he wants or to get what he wants. He will never keep his promises. To be honest I would not trust Frederick Southpool to tell me the time. The trouble is, he pays so well."

Hollis wrote in her notebook, "What is he like to work with?"

Samuel let out a sigh, "Dreadful. Frederick Southpool thinks that he is an inspired genius and that he is an inspirational leader. Working here is not easy. He believes that he could be the English Bill Gates or Steve Jobs. He cannot understand that those glory days have passed. Southpool Computing creates bespoke software packages for companies and Fred hates it. He loves the money but hates the fact that the company is just another small to medium sized business."

Hollis changed the direction of her questioning, "What's going on outside, in reception?"

Chappell was happy to let Hollis lead the interview while he sat and watched Samuel. It was clear that Samuel did not like his employer.

Samuel shifted in his chair and said, "Southpool Computing no longer exists in its present form. There has been a change of ownership. Fred Southpool sold shares in this business as a way of raising capital and he was unable to stop a takeover. The shares in this business have been snapped up. Fred Southpool has lost control of his company."

Hollis leant forward in her seat and asked, "When did he find out? How did he take it?"

Samuel gave a short laugh, "We found out last week, five days ago. How did he take it? He was livid. Crazy with anger. He couldn't believe it. It was like he couldn't believe that someone would dare to buy his company out from under him. He was in shock for a while and then just started throwing things around his office."

Hollis nodded and asked, "Does he normally lose his temper?"

Samuel shook his head, "No, no he doesn't. He is normally controlled, too controlled. I would call Frederick Southpool a cool character. You can tell that he is angry by the way he clenches his jaw or narrows his eyes at people. I call it cold fury. I've had enough meetings with him to know."

Chappell asked, "How come?"

Samuel turned to look at Chappell. He said, "Staff normally come to me with bad news and I seem to be the one to pass it on. There has been a lot of bad news recently. The takeover caused a lot of uncertainty and some of our main clients left us for other suppliers. Frederick tried hard to hang onto them. There has not been a good atmosphere over last few months.

Chappell commented, "Judging from what we heard outside, the staff seem happy with the takeover."

Samuel smiled, "The staff are very happy. Frederick Southpool is universally disliked by the staff at this company. He made staff work long hours and at weekends when he wanted them to. People were always one step away from being fired. Frederick reminded at least four people a day about their job contracts. He would make people cancel their holidays and then take off on holidays with his son, Robert at a moment's notice. Frederick trapped people with big salaries, some of the amounts are eye-wateringly big. Once you have that level of money coming in, it is hard to walk away."

Chappell asked, "What about you? Do you like him?"

Samuel Adesinsi raised his eyebrows, "I don't like him, but I got on with him. I am going to be the Managing Director of the new business. See that's another thing, Frederick called himself the President of the company. How can you be the president when you only have 150 staff? Delusions of grandeur. Let's just say I got on with Frederick, but his goal has always been making a fortune and spoiling his precious son."

Hollis asked, "What's Frederick Southpool like with women in general and the female staff at this business in particular?"

"He's very good looking but he just turns people off. The female staff don't like him. He has humiliated most of them at one time or another. I've been to a few conventions and exhibitions with him and yes, some women threw themselves at Frederick. He avoided them like the plague. I've only been aware of him having one or two girlfriends and they didn't stay with him for long. He is not very sympathetic. He is not comfortable showing any kind of emotion and he doesn't like spending money on people unless of course it's on his son."

Hollis was about to speak, Chappell interrupted her, "You've mentioned Frederick's Southpool's son three times now. Why?"

"Robert Southpool is, as the saying goes the apple

of his father's eye. Another saying says that the apple doesn't fall far from the tree. Robert Southpool has been spoilt by his father. That young man can do no wrong. If he wants money, his father gives it to him. Robert is trying to set up his own marketing business. His father expected all staff to work for Robert as well as doing their primary jobs. Honestly, neither the father nor son is well liked around here."

Hollis said, "What can you tell us about Jennifer Lindsay?"

"Ah, Jennifer, the beautiful Jennifer." Samuel gave them a beaming smile. "Jennifer is the future. She is definitely a world-class programmer. I am not exaggerating. When you see her work, it's not difficult to imagine her doing the same as Bill Gates and setting up her own business. She just possesses a kind of inspiration that I have not seen in anyone else. Her creativity and passion are, well, just amazing, absolutely amazing. I tell you she is like the Mozart of the computing world. She's a visionary. She came to us straight from university; Frederick was lucky to get her. I think that he must have promised her the moon, stars and the next universe to get her to come here. May I ask, why are you asking about her?"

Chappell coughed and answered, "Jennifer Lindsay was found drowned yesterday afternoon. She had gone out to the lake at Forge Tarn."

Silence filled the room. Samuel Adesinsi's mouth opened and closed, but no words came out. Chappell waited for Samuel to speak. Hollis observed Samuel. The smooth Mr Adesinsi had nothing to say. The veneer of sophistication vanished from Samuel's face. He started to look haggard and drained of all cheer.

At last when Samuel did speak it was to ask, "Is

she really dead? I mean you don't, you haven't mixed up her identity with someone else?"

Hollis repeated the information. "No, sadly, Jennifer Lindsay is now deceased."

"But then this company is dead too. Without her, this company is not worth having." Samuel put his elbows on his desk, closed his eyes and held his head. "This company is screwed. I am the Managing Director of nothing, nothing at all. I was about to set up a special projects department and she was to be one of the leaders of it."

Hollis questioned him further. "Surely you must have other staff who are just as good? How can you run a business with just one good employee?"

"You don't understand. Were you not listening? We have good programmers, excellent ones even, but I'm talking Mozart, Michelangelo, Da Vinci. She is, or rather was, one of a kind. Had she lived long enough she would have become a household name and she would have taken this company with her." Samuel raised his head and shrugged.

Chappell and Hollis exchanged looks. Chappell used his head to motion towards the door. Samuel Adesini was being over-dramatic. People did behave strangely when faced with unwelcome and shocking information.

Chappell said, "We have to go now sir. We will come back in due course."

"Yes, but what was she doing out there? There was no reason for her to be. I would have thought that she didn't want to be there."

"Why do you ask?"

"Because, because he fired her last week." Samuel sat up straight and stared at Chappell, his previous theatricality was forgotten. "Jennifer was getting ready to leave and had two or three job offers. She went to Frederick, asked for more money and the option to pick and choose the projects that she worked on. Not the best time to ask but she did anyway. He started shouting at her calling her a devious, underhanded backstabber. She was quite cheeky really. She didn't say anything while he was shouting at her and then she said, "So that's no then?" Frederick was so angry that he fired her on the spot. She just walked out, left all her stuff and walked out the door."

Hollis said, "If he fired her last week, how was it that she was going to be working for you?"

Samuel replied, "He fired her, I hired her. And now, well, that dream is over." Samuel shook his head. "I guess I'll have to start the search for another wonderkid. It will not be easy."

Hollis asked, "Would it have been possible for Southpool to have apologised to her and taken her out for a picnic to talk to her?"

Samuel shook his head, "I doubt it. I was there, at the meeting. It was ugly. Frederick's bad side came out. He used swear words that I'm not going to repeat, I didn't know that one person could fit so many swear words into one sentence. To paraphrase, he accused her of having no soul and no loyalty. That was rich coming from him. He could have been talking about himself. If you stand in his way or stand up to him, he will destroy you. There is no coming back. After what he said to her there was no way either one of them would go anywhere near each other. He was as mad as hell. Jennifer may have joked around but what he said to her to must have hurt. She was a kind soul. She would joke around but what he said to her that day was terrible."

Chappell raised an eyebrow, "How have you managed to survive working for him and stay on working for the new owners?"

Samuel grinned. "My role has included a lot of firefighting and keeping the peace. I am also the company accountant and I spent a lot of time telling him what we did have money for and what we didn't. Oh, there were arguments, but you can't argue with a lack of cash flow. Frederick cares about two things; the pursuit of riches and his precious son."

"You said that before."

"It's true. Frederick Southpool likes expensive things, the more expensive the better. One of the reasons that this company was in such a financial hole is because its owner used it as his personal piggy bank. I warned him so many times and still he took money out."

"Wasn't he committing criminal activity?" Hollis, who was keen to move into investigating white collar crime was interested.

Samuel shook his head, "No, Frederick was careful to stay on the right side of the law. That and the fact that I threatened him that I would report him if I thought he was embezzling from the company. What his love of money did, was to put pressure on the business. Every single contract mattered. Jennifer was the key to the business's success. She was not the only one, but she was able to come at a problem in a unique way. She was able to write programs that were so successful and efficient. Frederick wanted to work on a special project with her. He thought that it could put the company on the map after the share issue. That's probably another reason why he was so angry.

She knew what his idea was for the new software. She could probably have written it herself and sold it. If it was as good as he kept saying it was, it would have made her a lot of money."

Chappell said, "And Mr Southpool couldn't have written this software himself?"

Samuel said, "Frederick Southpool just isn't that good. The bottom line is that he was, and always will be a computer salesman. His programming skills are basic. Even the most junior programmer in this business is streaks ahead of him."

Chappell changed his mind about leaving. "Samuel, was there anyone here who was close to Jennifer? I'd like to speak to them if possible."

Samuel pulled a face and said, "Let's see, there is Marie Clarke. She and Jennifer have worked together on a few projects. Let me take you to the boardroom which is bigger and then I'll get her for you."

Chappell and Hollis were led along a short corridor which ended in a set of double doors. The room beyond them was painted white with a wall of large windows. A long black table was placed in the middle of the room and was surrounded by black leather chairs.

"Please wait here. Sit down if you wish." Samuel indicated the chairs and turned to leave.

Chappell called out, "Samuel, please don't tell her about the nature of our visit."

Hollis sat down and wrote up her notes while Chappell prowled around the room. He looked at pictures of Frederick Southpool meeting local and national dignitaries. Southpool was a short man who wore tortoise shell framed spectacles. His brown hair was cut long and flopped over his brow.

Other pictures showed Southpool on holiday in various locations. He was dressed in scuba diving gear and accompanied by a younger version of himself. This had to be his son, Robert. In one photograph both of them were holding conch shells, in another they were holding harpoons. In a third picture they were displaying a large swordfish, one was at the tail and the other at the sword. Father and son were happy, tanned and smiling for the camera.

Chappell turned and sat at the head of the table, "Hollis, what we have here is a puzzle." Chappell played idly with a coin that was on the table. "Jennifer was fired and a few days later she is having a picnic on the land of the man who just fired her. Why? What is it that we do not yet know?"

"A lot sir." Hollis could have pulled her tongue out. Chappell shot her a look of disbelief. "Sorry sir, it's just that I'm reviewing my notes. I have more questions than answers. Everyone we speak to adds to my list of questions."

"I feel the same way. Was Jennifer murdered by someone she knew or a stranger? A stranger would not have taken the time to stage that picnic. Why stage it at all? I keep coming back to that."

Chappell would have said more but he was interrupted by a knock at the door. Hollis stood up, opened the door and admitted Marie Clarke.

Marie was probably not even five feet tall. She wore a faded black Star Wars t-shirt featuring Han Solo and Princess Leia, a short black denim skirt, ripped black tights and red Converse boots with purple laces. Marie's make up consisted of chalk white foundation, black kohl eyeliner, black lipstick and chipped black nail varnish.

Marie had a soft quiet voice, "Hello, Samuel said you wanted to see me. He said that you are police officers?"

"Please come in, take a seat. I'm Detective Chief Inspector Chappell and this is Detective Sergeant Hollis." Chappell indicated the empty chair. Marie sat down and looked apprehensively at both the police officers.

Chappell began the questioning, "When we came in just now, I heard you call Frederick Southpool a lying, cheating bastard. You said that he had gambled and lost. Is that what you think has happened?"

"Hey, what's going on here?" Marie became agitated. "I just said that. I didn't mean anything by it. We all think that."

Chappell took the time to put Marie at her ease. He said, "Marie, we are not here to upset you but to carry out an investigation. Unfortunately, Jennifer Lindsay died yesterday."

"She what? She what?" Marie hung her head and started to rock in her chair. "No, no, she can't be dead. She's my friend. No, no, she just can't be. She just can't be." Marie paused, shaking her head as if she could refuse to accept what she had just been told. "And what was she doing with Mr Southpool? She hated him. He just fired her. No, it can't be." Marie started to cry.

Hollis spoke up. "Is there anything I can get you? A cup of tea, coffee?" Hollis handed a tissue. Marie blew her nose loudly and dried her eyes, smearing her black make up over her face.

Marie's voice was even quieter and more tremulous, "No, no thank you. It's just the shock. Sorry."

Chappell resumed. "There's absolutely no need to be sorry. I just wish that we were not the ones to break the news to you. I understand that you were good friends with Jennifer. I wonder if you could fill us in on her background and perhaps tell us why she may have been out with Mr Southpool."

Marie sniffed and dabbed at her eyes, "Why she was out with him, I have absolutely no idea. He fired her last week. The walls in this place are not the thickest so when she went to see him, we all heard about it. That man can swear I can tell you. If he said to me what he said to her you can bet, I'd just walk out and that is exactly what she did.

"In terms of working with her, she was a laugh. We all knew that she was way better than us at coding and software. She wasn't cocky about it though. If you had a problem, she would help you. She would help anyone. She got through her work far quicker than anyone else and she would just help people. She loved doing that." Marie paused, blinking back tears that threatened to fall. Hollis handed her some fresh tissues. Marie ignored the tissues and just let the tears fall. They traced grey rivulets on the black and white canvas of her face. The tears dripped unheeded from her cheeks onto her t-shirt.

Marie took a deep breath and continued in a soft low voice, "One thing I do know is, that Mr Southpool wanted her to work on some project with him. He wanted her to start it off and then the rest of us would have had to write some peripheral stuff. I know that she started working with him. He wanted her to come in at weekends and even go to his house. She wasn't keen on that, but she did want the project to succeed. That was until he fired her. After that she told him to stuff it and that the program was mainly hers anyway. He was ready to sue her for copyright, he told her that it was his intellectual property, she laughed and said how could he sue her for something that was in her head and that she hadn't written down anywhere?"

"How do you know this?" asked Hollis.

Marie replied, "On the day he fired her, Jennifer just left. She rang me and asked that I clear her desk and bring everything over to her house. I did that. When I saw her later, she said that Mr Southpool had been on the phone to her several times. In the end she just blocked his number and refused to answer the phone to any number she didn't know."

Chappell asked, "Do you think that he could have apologised to her and she accepted it?"

Marie shook her head vehemently. With a slightly stronger voice she said, "Mr Southpool does not apologise to people. There was no way back after what he said to Jennifer. Let me give you an example of what Mr Southpool is like. He stopped Samuel from going to a funeral for his uncle. He was really close to his uncle. Mr Southpool said to Samuel that his uncle was dead already, so he really wouldn't miss him at the funeral. It wasn't like Samuel had any big meetings or anything major to do that day, Frederick Southpool was just being bloody minded and nasty as usual."

Chappell asked, "What did Samuel do?"

"He called in sick and took a week off." Marie continued, "He came back with a doctor's note so there was nothing Mr Southpool could do about it."

Chappell said, "I guess you're happy Samuel is taking over here at the business?"

Marie nodded, "Yes, we all are. Samuel is really fair. He's a nice man. If the new owners will just let us get on, I think this company could grow and become something major. We'll need to get a new chief programmer though."

Chappell smiled and asked, "You don't want to go for the job?"

Marie shut her eyes and screwed her face up.

Chappell apologised, "I'm sorry, in the circumstances I should not have said that." Marie's vulnerability and pain at her friend's death was hard to watch. Chappell berated himself for his misplaced comment.

Marie nodded. "It's OK. I would never have gone for the job I'm not good enough." Marie wrapped her arms around her waist and sobbed. Her body was wracked by emotion. "Jennifer was my dearest friend, I'm going to miss her. This hurts so much."

Chappell and Hollis took their leave of Marie and Samuel and went back to the police station. Chappell massaged his temples; a headache was beginning to make its presence felt. It was a sure sign that he needed some coffee and the problem of Jennifer Lindsay's death was becoming more complex. He sat in his office with a fresh cup of bitter coffee and a clean sheet of paper. He thought about Jennifer Lindsay's death and started making notes.

He needed the coroner's report, but his personal opinion was that the young woman had been killed. Jennifer had been found in shallow water, if she had been conscious or alive she would have been able to move. He also needed the location of the primary crime scene. Was Jennifer killed beside the lake or elsewhere? Why was she moved? Would the location help to find the killer?

Chappell reviewed the information collected from the interviews he had carried out that day. Jack Danvers had seemed to be truthful and keen to move on with his life. His comments about Peter and Elle worried Chappell. Peter Riggs had appeared to be nothing except an extremely concerned friend. If Danvers was correct Peter had turned into the exact opposite. Could Peter have attacked Jennifer? Perhaps sick of Jennifer taking advantage of him, Peter could have snapped and decided to be a little more forceful with Jennifer. Perhaps she had fought him off, they struggled she fell, hit her head and died. Peter could then have bought some food and staged the scene by the lake.

Chappell ran a hand over his face as if washing it. Elle Latimer had lied about not knowing Lisa Blaine. Elle had lied about when she had returned home. What was she trying to cover up? If she had returned on Tuesday instead of Friday, she may well have had an argument with the unpredictable Jennifer. Jennifer's flirtation with Elle's colleague may not have gone down well, especially if Jennifer had done the same thing with a previous acquaintance of Elle's. Had Elle lied about the day she had returned home to cover for something Peter had done or to distance herself from something Peter had done? He looked at the notes he had made and added the name of Lisa Blaine. He wanted to interview the ex-girlfriend and find out just exactly why she had left Jennifer.

Leaving his office Chappell called over to Hollis, "I'd like to see Lisa Blaine. Do you have her details?" Hollis who had been chatting with Detective Lee Hudson at his desk returned to her own and picked up a sheet bearing the woman's details.

"Let's go Hollis. You can ring Ms Blaine on the way and tell her to expect us."

Chappell ran down the stairs, Hudson remarked, "It looks like action man is on to something, you'd better go."

Hollis nodded and ran after Chappell. The car was started and pointing out the police station car park by the time Hollis reached it. She gave Chappell the address and rang Lisa Blaine.

The door opened, "What are you doing in my room?" The hotel guest Rick Seers asked.

The duty manager said, "I'm sorry sir, I was just checking that your room was cleaned to our highest standard. We carry out spot checks just to make sure that guests have no complaints. I also came to place these in your room." The duty manager showed Mr Seers the small box of chocolates he was holding and placed them on the bedside table. The manager moved in such a way that his leg closed the drawer of the table he had been rifling through.

"Oh, ok thanks. Yes, you do have high standards in this hotel. I always enjoy staying here. Funny how I've never met one of you inspectors before though."

"We pride ourselves on not intruding on our guests. I try to do this when the hotel is quiet. I'll let myself out."

The duty manager was disappointed. A search of the room proved that Mr Seers was everything that he claimed to be; a businessman attending a conference where he was giving a few training sessions. No matter, there were a few other guests who would prove to be excellent targets. Henry Spires and

Miranda Holland had added to his nest egg.

Lisa Blaine lived in a quiet cobbled street. Her home was in a converted warehouse which housed six large apartments.

"This is an expensive part of town." Hollis looked around and back at the building where Lisa Blaine lived. "What on earth did Lisa and Jennifer have in common?"

Chappell walked up to the entry door, pushed a button, explained who he was and waited for the door to be opened. Chappell and Hollis took the lift to the third floor and walked along until they were met by a smiling woman, dressed in a navy blue suit with short bobbed hair.

"You're the police? I'm Lisa's sister, Louise. Don't ask, everyone in our family has a name beginning with an 'L'. Do come in Lisa will be along shortly."

The apartment was cavernous. There was no hall way, one simply entered into a large open plan space. Along one wall was a staircase which connected to a mezzanine floor. On the ground floor were a kitchen, dining area and a space with sofas and two high backed chairs. On the other side of the kitchen was a door which Louise explained led to a small bathroom and second bedroom. Chappell went off to use the bathroom and left Louise Blaine explaining the design features of the apartment to Hollis.

Chappell returned just in time to hear Louise explain that Lisa was an architect who worked in the same practice as Elle Latimer.

Hollis said, "I bet that could be awkward with Jennifer living in the same house as Elle."

Louise replied, "I don't really know. I don't live

here. I only drop in when I have meetings in the area."

Chappell asked, "What do you do?"

"I'm a project manager. If I've work up in this part of the world I stay with my accommodating baby sister."

Louise directed the police officers to sit down whilst they waited for Lisa. Chappell and Hollis did not have to wait long before Lisa Blaine returned home. The resemblance between the sisters was striking. They could have been twins. Lisa was dressed in a chunky cream coloured jumper which was tucked into a brown skirt covered with a flower design. She finished the look with a pair of high heeled brown suede boots. She had the same bobbed hair cut as her sister. The haircut accented the sharp cheekbones that both women possessed.

Louise laughed easily as she saw the looks of confusion on the police officers' faces. "No, we are not twins, there is three years between us."

Louise turned to her sister, "Are you going to be alright? Do you want me to stay?"

"No Louise, you go. You've got to catch your train. I'll ring you later."

Louise Blaine nodded to Hollis and Chappell picked up her bag and coat that had been draped over a chair and left the flat.

Lisa turned to the police officers, "Would you like some tea or coffee."

"Coffee would be just fine," Chappell volunteered.

"Some tea for me please," Hollis replied.

Lisa busied herself filling the two requests, "Can you tell me why you have come to see me?"

Chappell spoke up, "I understand that you recently

split up with Jennifer Lindsay. I wanted to ask you about that and about your movements in the past few days."

Lisa called out to Hollis, "Do you take milk and sugar in your tea?"

"Just milk, no sugar." Lisa finished making the drink and handed a mug to Hollis.

"And you, Detective Chief Inspector, how do you take your coffee?"

"No sugar and just a dash of milk."

"Good man, that's how I drink it myself."

Lisa handed Chappell his drink. He sipped it, "This is good." He took another sip, "This is really good. You'll have to tell which beans you use. I'm impressed."

Lisa smiled, "I certainly will. As to your questions, I'll answer the easiest one first. I've been in Denmark for the past few days. I got back yesterday. If you need any proof my airline ticket is on the table." She sorted through a pile of papers on her dining table and gave her boarding card stub to Chappell. He looked at it and smiled. Lisa sat down.

Hollis asked, "Did Elle Latimer travel with you?"

"No, she should have been here in town at the office. She shouldn't have been travelling anywhere. She's had a few meetings with clients and contractors but nothing that would have required her to stay away from home on business matters.

"Now, I guess you want to know about Jennifer and myself." Lisa sighed deeply and took a gulp of her coffee. "What can I say, it was a mistake. I fell for Jennifer and she fell for me. I spent the last few months trying to extricate myself from the relationship and I told her quite a few times that everything was over, but she would not take no for an answer. I know that Peter, if you ask him will say that he and Jennifer caught me sneaking about having dinner with someone else. The thing is I wasn't sneaking or cheating or doing anything underhand. I had told Jennifer that things were over and that I had moved on. She just didn't believe me."

Chappell asked, "What did she do when she saw you together?"

Lisa spoke with a sad resigned tone, "At first, she walked out of the restaurant and then rang me to rant and swear at me. After that she bombarded me with text messages all accusing me of cheating on her. When she calmed down she sent me pleading messages and left voice mails asking to meet up and just have one last meeting."

Chappell asked, "Did you meet her?"

Lisa nodded, "Yes, out by the lake at Forge Tarn. She had a really ugly black eye. I asked her about how she got it. She mistook my concern for her injury and assumed that I wanted to get back together with her. I just had to walk away from her. I feel so sorry. I walked away from her and I understand that she was found drowned in the lake. The trouble is Jennifer could be so clingy and insecure. I was fed up of having to be the strong one."

Chappell asked, "Was that the last time that you saw or heard from her?

Lisa nodded, "The last time I saw her definitely, I had a few more text messages from her."

Chappell moved the questioning onto a different topic, "How did Jennifer's behaviour affect your new relationship?"

Lisa raised her eyebrows and said, "It hasn't. Or

perhaps I should say that I decided that I ought to take some time for myself, so I called things off and I'm enjoying the single life right now."

Chappell asked, "You seem so much older than Jennifer, how did the two of you get together in the first place?"

Lisa shrugged, "I have no idea. Truly, it's something that I have thought long and hard about over the past few months. I think that we had something that should have remained as a quick fling. It turned into something else and Jennifer put far more effort into the relationship than I was prepared to do."

Hollis asked, "Did the relationship cause friction between you and Elle Latimer?"

Lisa shook her head, "I shouldn't have thought so. I'm Elle's boss. I think for a while she thought that Jennifer was going to tell me everything that she got up to. Jennifer didn't and I didn't ask Jennifer about Elle either."

Chappell said, "Well, thank you. Great coffee."

Lisa stood up, grabbed a pen and wrote something down on a sheet of paper. She gave it to Chappell. "That's the name of the coffee and where you can buy it. Not many places sell it I'm afraid."

The sun set, colouring the sky muted shades of red and purple. Chappell and Hollis were soon back at the squat red brick police station. It provided Chappell with a sense of solidity in this otherwise confusing case. His headache was back, almost blinding him with its intensity. He was thankful for the dull uninspiring décor of the police station. The municipal greys and browns relaxed him even if normally, he wondered why more cheerful colours could not be used.

The police team tucked into the pizzas Chappell had provided for them. The team, like Chappell, were feeling stumped.

"Everyone, I think that you should take a break, go to the gym or get some sleep or do both." Chappell paused, "Of course, I do need a volunteer to stay behind and cover the office."

Chappell looked around, making eye contact with each team member. "No volunteers? I'll have to pick someone, you know that, right?"

"I'll do it." Hollis spoke up. "I'll do it."

Lee Hudson shouted out, "Well done Hollis."

After her colleagues left, Hollis sent a message to her boyfriend cancelling yet another date. She then walked over to the whiteboard and stared at the photographs and reports that had been pinned up. She looked at the timeline that started with the reporting of the death and ended with their current interviews and investigations. She unpinned a large photograph of Jennifer. She spoke aloud.

"Who are you? What happened to you? Why did someone kill you?"

Taking his own advice, Mike Chappell had visited the gym and had gone home. He too spent the evening reviewing the information collected so far on the death of Jennifer Lindsay. Something dark lay at the heart of Jennifer Lindsay's death, he had no evidence for this, and it frustrated him. He just needed one loose thread to pull and thereby unravel the case.

He read the pathology report. It indicated that Jennifer had been strangled and she was dead before she went into the water. The time of death could not be specified but it had probably taken place within a six hour window. There was no water in her lungs. There was also no food in her stomach apart from the remains of a partially digested croissant. Jennifer had not engaged in any consensual sexual activity neither had she been the subject of a sexual attack. Perhaps the most important point was that Jennifer Lindsay had no alcohol in her system.

It was murder. Jennifer Lindsay was now the victim of murder. The team would need to investigate deeper into the people who had been questioned. They would also have to question people who had been tangential to the investigation. What was Jennifer's relationship with Frederick Southpool? Who else had Jennifer angered over the past few weeks?

The photos of Jennifer revealed nothing surprising. Apart from the ugly bruises around her neck, she bore no other wounds or marks. Jennifer had been dressed in a purple sweatshirt and black jeans. She had worn black boots with flat heels and large buckles on the ankles. Her other personal effects included her telephone and purse. These had been jammed into the back pockets of her jeans and had therefore remained in place when thrown into the water. The phone was water logged and unusable. A request had been put in for the phone records, but they had yet to arrive.

Chappell reviewed the rest of the photos especially the ones of the food laid out on the bank of the lake, resting on a plastic bag. There was a packet of six sausage rolls, there were six sausage rolls evident. Another packet contained four pork and cranberry pies, there were two pies lying on the grass on top of a slip of paper. He studied the food packets and the label on the wine bottle. All of the food came from a well-known supermarket. Chappell recalled that there was a branch not too far from the lake.

It was nearly midnight. Chappell headed for his bed but not to sleep. From experience, he knew that he would not rest properly until the case was solved.

At midnight Hollis was still at her desk focusing on Jennifer's murder. Her phone buzzed yet again. A text message flashed up. It was from Simon, her boyfriend. He had sent five messages telling her how angry he was that she kept cancelling on him. Laura had not replied to a single one. This last message, the sixth was to tell her that he was finishing with her. To this message she replied, "Fine. Goodbye. Have a nice life."

Nothing in her life meant more to her than her job. She enjoyed looking for evidence, making connections and catching suspects. No relationship brought her that much of a thrill. Simon was better off without her.

Chappell strode into his office with his obligatory cup of coffee in hand. He set about finding the answers to his questions. He read over the initial report that Frederick Southpool had made and compared it with the information given to him by Officer Barnes. Frederick Southpool had not started to give his report until 3.40 pm. Why did he wait so long? The information from Samuel Adesinsi was quite damming about Southpool's character. Frederick Southpool was definitely a line of investigation that needed to be followed up. There were quite a few questions that needed to be asked of that man. Chappell also wanted to get to the bottom of the evasiveness shown by Elle Latimer and Peter Riggs.

Hollis walked into the Chappell's office with a sheaf of papers, "The IT guys have started work on Jennifer Lindsay's computer. Apparently they agree that she is a genius. They couldn't make much sense of some of the programs that she was writing but looking at all the other information on her hard drive she seemed to have normal preoccupations. It looks like she looked up shopping sites, emailed a few people and had been working on find a new job. She does not appear to have wanted to blackmail anyone nor was she keeping any secret information."

"Take a seat Hollis. Let's discuss this case. I take it you spent some time reviewing the notes last night?"

Hollis sat down, "Yes. I did."

Chappell asked, "So why was she killed Hollis? Is this an accidental death and if so why not just leave her where she died? Who would move the body, place it in the water where it was bound to be found and then stage that picnic?"

"For my money, I'd say it was Peter Riggs. One minute he's acting like some lovesick fool and the next he's practically abandoning her, leaving her to make her own way home. What if he told her how he felt about her, and she just laughs in his face? He snaps, grabs her and strangles her. Now she's dead he bundles her into his car drives over to the lake and dumps her body."

"But Hollis, we've already established that dumping the body would be difficult. There were no tyre tracks there before the forensic team arrived. Peter would have needed to have parked in the car park at the other end of the lake and carried the body to where it was found. There was only one rowing boat and that was chained up."

"It could have floated over to the other side." Hollis knew her point was weak, but she felt that Peter Riggs was responsible for the death. She continued her argument, "So alright, I don't know why someone apart from Peter would care enough to make out that she was having a picnic? Jack's moved out and has several witnesses as to his whereabouts. That leaves Elle. She could have killed Jennifer and moved the body, but I think it highly unlikely. In either case, if they were going to commit a murder I don't see them setting the scene so meticulously."

Chappell nodded and said, "It's this scene setting that we keep coming back to." Chappell held his hand out for the documents Hollis was holding. "Find out where the architectural practice is. I am not happy that Elle Latimer lied to us. I think we will pay her a visit and speak to her colleague Andy at the same time. First though, I think we should see Mr Southpool."

The bar of the Twelve Kings Hotel was the same as could be found in many mid-priced hotels. There were a lot of tinted mirrors and spotlights. The tables were of brown flecked glass accompanied by chairs covered in rough brown fabric. The few windows that there were looked out over the hotel's carpark. The bar was empty except for the Frederick Southpool and the duty manager who was currently doubling up as the barman.

Frederick Southpool was talking with a young man when Chappell and Hollis arrived. As soon as he noticed the police officers Southpool patted the young man on the back and they parted company. Southpool walked towards the police officers whilst the young man headed towards an exit at the rear of the bar leading to the carpark. He was wearing what seemed to be his normal attire; black top and jeans.

Southpool's manner was calm and polite. He made no mention of the man with whom he had been speaking. Before reaching the exit, the young man glanced around. Hollis caught a brief look at him in one of the many mirrors. The young man resembled Southpool so, it was probably his son.

Southpool said, "You are Detective Chief Inspector Chappell and Detective Sergeant Hollis? I've been expecting you. Is there anything I can get you? Tea, coffee, anything?"

"Was that your son, who just left, Mr Southpool?"

"Yes, yes it is." Southpool turned around and looked at the far exit through which his son had left. A faint smile on his face.

Chappell said, "Mr Southpool, I'll have a coffee, but we will have to pay for our own drinks. Thank you all the same." Southpool crossed to the bar counter and placed the order and returned to sit down.

He assessed Frederick Southpool. There was nothing about the man before him that bore any similarity to the man described to them back at Southpool Computing. Once the beverages were on the table, Chappell began his questioning.

Chappell started with the question that had been troubling him the most. "Mr Southpool, I have to say I am struck by the fact that you found a body in a lake on your land and drove all the way over here to tell us. Why did you not ring?"

Southpool raised his hands palms up, "My mobile was flat, completely out of juice. I put myself through a punishing running schedule, I did ten miles on Sunday morning. The only thing that kept me going was the playlist on my phone. I had my earphones in and off I went."

Chappell continued his questioning, "I can understand that, I'm exactly like that but why didn't you ring from your house phone. You ran home why not go and use your landline?"

Southpool shrugged, "I don't know. I think I was on automatic. I just kept thinking I must tell the police; I must tell the police. I know that your police station is the largest in the area, so I just drove over here."

"And then you sat down and waited your turn. Why not just go up to the desk and announce your problem?"

Southpool looked from Chappell to Hollis and back to Chappell. He said, "I've thought about all of this. I really don't know. I had just seen a dead body. A dead body in a lake near my home. I mean that is the place that I live. I think that I was just trying to process all of that and the fact that it was someone I knew. I just knew it had to be Jennifer. I was thinking about that focusing on only that."

Hollis said, "I was going to ask you about that. We understand that you fired her and then tried to get her to come back. When that didn't work you threatened her with a lawsuit. Could you tell us about that?"

"Wow, you have been doing your digging."

Chappell frowned at Southpool and said, "This is a murder inquiry Mr Southpool, we will investigate, and we will do so thoroughly. So, please tell us."

"You probably know by now that I have been ousted from the company that I set up." Chappell nodded. "I can't say that my temperament was at its best over the last few months. I look back now and I realise that I must have been a monster to work with. Well Jennifer was toying with the idea of leaving and asked me for a raise. The business didn't have any money. I was actively searching for more capital. When she asked for more money I just told her to leave." Southpool gave a rueful smile, "I admit that my language was not the best and I probably used every swear word I knew but I couldn't believe that she was ready to jump ship.

"Anyway, she walked out. When I realised what I had done I tried to apologise and get her to come back. She didn't want to have anything to do with me. I'm not surprised really but I just wanted to say sorry. As for the lawsuit, we were working on a project developing a new program that would have been revolutionary. I will admit that her programming skills are far better than mine and that is why I had her working on it. The trouble is the program was mostly in her head and you can't sue a person for what is contained within their brain and not written down anywhere. So, at the moment I'm here trying to drum up some capital to start a new business. I'll have to hire some new staff and see if I can't get my idea off the ground."

Chappell nodded, he said, "Why was your son visiting you here?"

Both Chappell and Hollis had been watching Southpool intently throughout the interview. They saw annoyance race across Southpool's face just before he cleared his throat and swallowed.

Southpool said, "He came to see how I was."

Keeping to a conversational tone, Hollis asked, "What does he do?"

Southpool smiled again. The smile did not reach his eyes. He said, "Oh, he works in marketing, he has a small agency. He has done some work for me in the past and now I want him to join me with my new venture." Southpool shifted in his seat and cleared his throat.

Chappell nodded, and said, "What was Jennifer doing on your land?"

The abrupt changes in questioning left Southpool confused. He stammered his answer, "I.. I let her. She loved the pub and the lake. She said that she found it really peaceful out by the lake and that she got some of her best ideas just sitting by the water. I'm all for good ideas and if sitting beside a lake was all it took to get the program I wanted out of her, so much the better."

Hollis asked, "Why do you think she still continued to do so even after you fired her?"

Southpool gave another of his practiced smiles, looked Hollis full in the face and said, "My secret hope is that she was working on the program and that she would have come back to talk to me when it needed to be run in a lab. I hoped that I had piqued her interest. It's all well and good having an idea and running it on one computer but she would have needed access to more facilities in order to test it and to debug it. That was my hope. Now I'll never know."

Chappell sat back in his chair and looked at Frederick Southpool. The policeman was quite open about his observation. Hollis remained silent.

Needing to fill the silence, Southpool said, "Is there anything else?"

Chappell asked, "Did your son ever have anything to do with Jennifer Lindsay?"

Southpool's cheeks flushed. "No, I mean yes. I mean he didn't have that much to do with her, but he did stop by the office every so often to see me. There were a few times when Jennifer and I were working at my home and he'd be there, but I think that that was all. Are you suggesting that Robert could be involved? I mean really you can't believe that..."

With another change of direction, Chappell asked "Is there anything you can tell us that you think might be relevant to this investigation?"

Southpool regained his composure and replied, "No sorry I don't think so. Believe me, I have been thinking. At the end of the day, one of my ex-employees is found by me in a lake on my land. I know that it doesn't look good for me, but I had absolutely no reason to kill her. I needed her alive and working for me. I'm sorry, is there anything else? I have a meeting in a few minutes."

Hollis asked yet another unrelated question, "Mr Southpool why are you staying here?"

"That's easy, the company has an account here. We keep a few rooms for those people who have meetings and don't want to travel home. I'm staying here because I didn't want to go back to my house. I've been in and out of here for the past week, but I've stayed here continuously since I came to report the death of Jennifer."

There was a crash of smashed glass. The barman now back behind the bar had dropped a wine glass he had been polishing onto the brown marble countertop.

"I'm sorry for the disturbance," said the barman.

Chappell said, "Thank you for your time Mr Southpool. One last question, you no longer work for the company, how is it that you are using the company account?"

"I think that it is a courtesy. They are letting me use the hotel as a base while I sort myself out and find my feet again. You must excuse me; I need to get ready for my meeting."

Frederick Southpool rose from the table and walked quickly out of the bar. Chappell and Hollis followed him out of the bar, walked out of the hotel and back to the police station.

Chappell frowned and sighed. He sighed again and shook his head.

"You don't seem happy, sir. What is it about him that troubles you? He gave a plausible account of himself."

"That's just it Hollis, he gave a plausible account." Chappell answered, speaking his thoughts out aloud. "Was it true? He said all the right things, but they don't feel right. There is something about that man that isn't right. I understand exactly what Officer Barnes meant about him. The man is too controlled and too happy to help. The picture we have of him from the people at Southpool Computing does not match the impression that he just gave us."

Hollis agreed. She added, "Yes, especially when you asked him those unexpected questions. He just became flustered. I would add him to our list of possible suspects, apart from the fact that he needed Jennifer alive so that she could work on his program."

The duty manager took a long drag on his cigarette. He let the nicotine fill his lungs. He held his breath for a few moments and expelled the smoke through his nose. He took another drag and repeated the action. He would be back on duty in thirty minutes, just enough time to check up on the new guests.

Being an unobtrusive member of staff in a hotel meant that people ignored you. They carried on their conversations believing that they could not be heard, or at least the polite staff member would be discreet. They were wrong. There were a few things that he had heard earlier that day that he knew could not be true. Where there was a lie, there was money to be made.

Blue, Williams and Orell Architects was a medium sized business housed in a modern tower block in Bristol. Chappell approached the reception desk, introduced himself and asked to see Ms Elle Latimer. He was told that Ms Latimer was in a meeting and could not be disturbed. Chappell looked stony faced at the receptionist.

He leant forward slightly, narrowed his eyes and spoke in a slow even tone, "Young lady, Ms Latimer can be disturbed, and she will be disturbed. I wish to speak with her now. Is Ms Blaine in?"

The receptionist blanched. "Ah…yes she is".

"Please tell Ms Blaine that we are here, and we wish to speak with Ms Latimer."

The receptionist picked up her telephone and mumbled into it.

The receptionist said, "Ms Blaine will see you now Detective Chief Inspector Chappell. Please take the lifts over there."

Lisa Blaine was standing by an open office when Chappell and Hollis exited from the lift.

"Chief Inspector, Sergeant what is this about?"

Chappell answered, "Ms Blaine it's about gaining some clarity in the investigation of Jennifer's death. May we go into the office?"

Lisa stood aside and let the police officers enter.

"Ms Blaine, please take a seat." Lisa did so. Chappell continued, "Unfortunately I must report that there is no doubt that Jennifer was murdered on Sunday. Right now, all we can say is by person or persons unknown."

Lisa's face hardened, her eyelids closed, and her hands clenched into fists. "And you suspect me, is that it?"

"No Lisa, we do not suspect you. You say you were not in the country and I am sure that the Danish police will verify that fact. I'm here to question Elle Latimer and you have someone on your staff called Andy. We'd like to question him too."

Lisa sat stunned, head lowered, mouth opening and closing silently.

"Detective Chappell, is this all because I split up with Jennifer? Would she still be alive if we…if I had walked away?"

Chappell replied, "Lisa, I do not know but I doubt it. I don't wish to be blunt, but someone killed her and whether accidently or on purpose remains to be seen but I doubt that the state of your relationship had anything to do with it."

Lisa nodded, "She was a good person. I just didn't want to be with her. My feelings had changed." She swallowed a sob and looked up glassy eyed at

Chappell and Hollis. "I will do whatever I can to help you. I'll take you to one of the meeting rooms and send Elle and Andrew along."

Hollis asked, "What is Andrew's surname?"

"Grinner. Andrew Grinner."

Lisa stood and left the office. She walked along a grey carpeted hall whose walls were decorated with abstract prints of architectural features. Some were of the struts of bridges while others were of the roofs of buildings. Chappell looked at them momentarily, they reminded of the mountains he had climbed.

"If you wait in here, I'll go and get Elle and Andrew. Do you want to see both together or separately?"

"Together to begin with. Thank you."

The meeting room contained a round table with four chairs, telephone conferencing equipment and a television screen. In the corner was a scale model of an office block designed and built by the firm. Hollis studied this while Chappell took a seat at the table and read through his notebook. They did not have to wait long for Elle and Andrew to arrive.

Hollis deliberately took a seat directly opposite Chappell. It of course meant, that Elle and Andrew would be sat between the two police officers and opposite each other.

Chappell began the questioning, "Ms Latimer and Mr Grinner. Unfortunately, I have the sad task of telling you that Jennifer Lindsay was murdered. She was deliberately killed. You two may be among the last people to see her alive. Mr Grinner, may I call you Andy?"

The young man nodded. He looked ill. His Adam's apple bobbed up and down his throat several times.

"So, Andy you were at Ms Latimer's home on which day last week?"

"Ah…it was Tuesday. Yes, Tuesday. Elle had a meeting in Bath, and she had left a drawing which we needed to show a client on Wednesday. I said I'd go around and collect the drawing and do some work on it on Tuesday evening."

"Who did meet when you got to the house?"

"Well that guy Jack. He was packing to move, and we got talking. He asked me to help him move a few things into his van. I helped him do that." Andy swallowed nervously.

"And then?"

"And then, I…I met Jennifer. She was there and chatted to Jack and me about stuff really. She made me a cup of tea and we had a good chat and I lost track of time. Next thing I know Elle had returned home and I had spent several hours talking to Jennifer. That was the first and last time I met Jennifer."

"What did you talk about?"

"I dunno. I mean which pubs and clubs we went to, best place to get a kebab after a night out and things like that. Nothing serious."

As Andy spoke, Hollis watched Elle's expression. Elle was staring intently at Andy. It seemed as if she wanted him to stop talking but Andy was suffering from that volubility that some people suffer from when being questioned by the police. Elle moved her legs and would have kicked Andy under the table if Hollis had not caught her eye.

Chappell continued with his questions, "About what time would you say Ms Latimer returned home that evening?"

"Oh, I would say about seven. That's about right wouldn't you say Elle, seven?" Elle nodded and looked up at the ceiling. Andy continued, "Yes about seven. I don't think that Elle expected me to still be there, so I just took the drawing off the table and left."

"Well thank you Andy you have been extremely helpful. I think that's all. Detective Sergeant Hollis do you have any further questions?"

"No, I don't. Let me see you out." Hollis rose, walked over to the door and held it open for Andy Grinner. She closed the door behind him and retook her seat.

Chappell stared at Elle, placed his elbows on the table and steepled his hands. He rested his chin on his hands. He sat in silence, allowing the silence to make Elle Latimer uncomfortable. She shifted in her seat and pressed her lips together. She began to pluck at her top and to look around the room. She looked anywhere but at Chappell and Hollis.

"Elle, I would like some clarity from you." Chappell looked at his notebook and up at Elle. "When we spoke to you earlier you said that you returned home on Friday and gave the impression that you had been traveling on business. Mr Grinner and Ms Blaine tell us that you may have had to travel to business meetings but none of them required overnight stays or foreign travel. Please can you explain yourself?"

Elle tried to shrug but her haunted look belied the movement. "Did I say that? It must have been a mistake."

"No, I don't think so. At first you said Thursday and you corrected yourself and said Friday. You wanted to give the impression that you had not been at home last week and now your housemate is dead. What do you know about her murder? Maybe you murdered her yourself?"

"Now look here." Elle jumped out of her chair. "You can't say that to me!"

"Sit down." Chappell spoke. His voice was cold and unforgiving. "Sit down and stop being so melodramatic. Lying to the police and wasting our time is an offence. Would you like to be led out of this building in handcuffs and arrested?"

Elle returned to her seat. Her face now bore a fearful expression. Hollis permitted herself a small smile. Hollis enjoyed watching Chappell cut witnesses down to size.

"Ms Latimer I will start again. You made a point in telling us that you had not returned home until Friday. Andy tells us that you were at home on Tuesday when Jennifer was present. Mr Danvers tells us that you were expected back that day. Ms Blaine tells us that there was no reason for you to have been travelling any long distances for business. Explain yourself, otherwise we will have to arrest you."

Elle looked at Chappell then Hollis and back to Chappell.

"I won't say a thing. My movements are my own. Yes, I came back on Tuesday and then I left again almost immediately. I came back on Friday as I said."

"What did you do on the intervening two days?"

Elle shook her head and looked at the table.

Chappell let out a snort of exasperation, "Hollis, arrest Ms Latimer, charge her with obstruction of justice and for aiding and abetting a criminal."

Hollis stood behind Elle, "Ms Latimer please stand

up and place your hands out in front of you." Hollis removed a set of plastic cuffs from a pocket, "Ms Elle Latimer, you are being arrested on the charge of….."

Hollis unfurled the restraint and slowly began to slide it around Elle's wrists.

"This can't be happening. You can't be doing this."

Hollis paused in doing up the handcuffs.

Elle's eyes started to water, "No, no wait. I'll tell you. I can't believe this is happening." Elle burst into tears, she took a number of deep breaths and continued to sob. "How can this be happening to me? I have been going to work and I did have some meetings."

Hollis gently guided Elle back into her seat.

"The thing is that I'm having an affair with Mr Orell, one of the partners of this firm. I have been for some time now. Nobody knows. I spend some evenings at the house and some evenings with him. He has separated from his wife and they are getting divorced, but we just didn't want anyone to know about it. Adam, Mr Orell has an apartment in Bristol, and I spent Tuesday, Wednesday and Thursday evenings there. I have been coming to work as normal. We don't see each other during the day and we just meet up at night."

Chappell nodded, "And the weekend, last weekend when Jennifer died?"

"I came back to the house on Friday like I said but I didn't see Jennifer. I don't know if she was in or not. I came back, had a drink with Peter in the lounge and had a bath. On Saturday I met up with some friends and didn't come back until the early hours. Yes, I can give you their names if you want. On

Sunday I stayed in bed late, got up, did some laundry and not much else."

Chappell was remorseless in his questioning. He looked at Elle Latimer with disdain. He asked, "Why did you say that you did not know who Jennifer's girlfriend was?"

Elle shook her head and said, "I didn't want to get involved. How could I say that Jennifer's girlfriend was my boss? I thought that if I didn't say anything, you'd go away."

Chappell said, "But here we are again with more questions, treating you as a person of interest. Detective Sergeant Hollis, please go and see if Mr Orell is on the premises. Please tell him that we wish to question him immediately." Hollis acknowledged the order and went off in search of the man.

Elle took several deep breaths and said, "Detective Chief Inspector Chappell do you really need to do this. I've told you everything now."

"Ms Latimer, your housemate is dead. You have not shown an ounce of concern. Instead you are more interested in keeping your secrets."

A note of pleading crept into Elle's voice as she said, "I'm not a hypocrite. Jennifer made a point of flirting with my friends, both male and female. She made me feel uncomfortable and she knew it. I didn't like her. I didn't want her dead, but I just wanted her to leave my friends and myself alone. You don't need to speak to Adam."

Hollis returned followed by a slim muscular man of medium height, wearing a turquoise coloured polo shirt and black jeans. His dark curly hair was greying at the temples. Hollis introduced him to Chappell, "Mr Adam Orell this is Detective Chief Inspector

Chappell."

Chappell stood and pointed to a chair, "Please be seated Mr Orell. Ms Latimer you can go."

"Oh but…" Elle looked helplessly at Adam Orell as she was escorted from the room by Hollis.

Adam twisted in his chair to look at Elle and would have risen if Chappell had not said, "Please remain in your chair Mr Orell."

"Now see here Detective, I really don't see what this has got to do with Elle or me. What's the point of all this?" Adam curled his hands into fists and rested them on the table. His face reddened as he stared at Chappell.

Hollis re-entered and took a seat.

Ignoring Orell, Chappell asked, "Everything alright out there Hollis?"

Hollis nodded, "Yes sir, I told Ms Latimer not to leave the building in case we needed to speak to her again."

Orell uncurled his hands and began drumming his fingers on the table top. He said, "I've already asked you, what is this to do with us?"

"Mr Orell, we are investigating the death of Jennifer Lindsay. Ms Lindsay was a housemate of Ms Latimer's. Please can you tell me what you know of Ms Latimer's movements over the last week? I would appreciate candour and truthfulness. We have a lot to do and not a lot of time?"

"What can I tell you? Elle and I are seeing each other. I have separated from my wife and am waiting for the divorce to be finalised. Elle spends some evenings with me and some back at her own home. I'd like her to move in full-time but she's not ready for that yet."

Hollis asked, "Where is your wife? What does she think of Elle?"

Orell shrugged, "Oh, she's back in the States. When I moved over here she didn't want to come. I tried the whole transatlantic thing for a while, but it didn't work out. Elle has nothing to do with my divorce. I got to know her over the last few years and I really love being around her. Look I'm sorry that her housemate is dead, but Elle had nothing to do with it. I'm sure of that."

Chappell said, "Mr Orell, I find it a stretch of coincidence to find out that Ms Blaine had a relationship with Jennifer Lindsay, and you are having a relationship with Elle Latimer. How is it that both women lived in the same house?"

"I think that's a bit cart before the horse. Their house is where I met Elle socially for the first time. I mean Lisa was dating Jennifer and I dropped her off at Jennifer's home. I was there when Elle came home and all four of us went out for a drink. Things just developed from there. Is it possible to keep this quiet? The only person who knows anything about this is Lisa. Could we keep it that way?"

Chappell looked at his notes and back at Adam Orell.

Orell said, "Well, you wanted candour, I'm being candid."

Chappell frowned, "If it has no bearing on the case then yes, we will try to keep it quiet. Thank you Mr Orell."

After Orell left, Chappell remained at the table. He made some notes, threw his pen down and massaged his temples.

"You probably need some coffee, sir." Hollis

stood, "I noticed a coffee shop next door. We could go and sit in there?"

"Good thinking Hollis. It's not really the caffeine, I need to try to find a loose end. If Elle Latimer didn't do it, who did?"

"Sir, I have a theory that it was Peter Riggs."

"Why? Why him? I need evidence Hollis, not a theory or a gut instinct. What evidence do we have that it was any one of the people that we have interviewed so far?"

"None, sir."

Chappell continued massaging his temples as he said, "There's some intelligence behind this death. Come on, let's get that coffee and then we can visit your chief suspect. You can interview him."

Peter Riggs opened the front door and took a seat in the lounge. His eyes were still red, and his nose was streaming from a cold.

Hollis was straight to the point with her questioning, "Peter, the last time we spoke you led us to believe that you were Jennifer's best friend and that you cared deeply for her. Wouldn't it be fair to say that over the last few weeks Jennifer cared very little for you and you were becoming obsessed with her?"

"Yes." Peter whispered his answer, his mouth barely opened. "Yes, it's true."

Hollis warmed to her theme as she said, "Is that true enough for you to have killed her?"

"But I didn't. Oh, I don't know perhaps I did. I don't know. I don't know. Is it my fault she's dead? Did I kill her?"

Hollis did not expect Peter to admit anything so quickly and even Chappell was caught off-guard.

Chappell signalled to Hollis that he would take over the questioning. He used a low gentle tone, conscious as he was that Peter seemed close to another bout of crying.

"Peter, could you explain yourself. Why are you blaming yourself for Jennifer's death? What did you do?"

"Nothing, that's just it. I did absolutely nothing and now she's dead. Perhaps if I had done something she would still be alive."

Chappell asked, "What is it you think you should have done but didn't do?"

"I didn't go and collect her. She wanted a lift from somewhere and asked me to collect her. When she asked I didn't particularly listen and all I said was "I'll see." I wasn't busy or anything I was just sick and tired of her asking me for lifts to go to places. It wasn't that she wanted to spend time with me just wanted me to do her shopping and drive her about. I finally realised that she was just using me, and I wasn't going to do it any longer."

Chappell asked, "So, do you remember where she wanted you to collect her from and when?"

Peter shook his head. Tears ran down his cheeks. "No, that's it, I just told you I didn't listen, and I didn't care."

Chappell spoke slowly as if trying to calm an upset child, "Peter was she here on Saturday?"

Peter wiped at his face as he said, "At some point. I think that she came back late on Saturday, had some breakfast on Sunday morning and went out to meet someone. I don't know who or where. I didn't listen. I told her to catch a bus and I'd see if I was free in the afternoon to collect her. The thing is, I totally forgot and didn't care. She even called me a few times. As soon as I saw it was her I didn't answer the phone and I deleted her voice messages without listening to them. I didn't even remember anything about her needing to come home until the policeman came and said she was dead.

"So, can't you understand?" Peter continued, "Maybe I killed her. If I had gone to get her. If I had remembered or even listened to her I might be able to tell you who it was that she went to meet. She just made me so angry." Peter wiped his nose with his hand and started weeping.

Back in the incident room, Chappell called the team together to review their investigation. Jennifer Lindsay had a tidy sum of money in both her current and savings accounts. She was not extravagant in her spending, but she did like expensive clothes, shoes and bags. Clothing and accessories which she could well afford. She also spent money on top of the range computer equipment, again she could afford to do so. She was not in debt and her credit card was paid up. If she kept a diary it was neither electronic nor written down. The last email she had sent was to accept a job offer from a computing firm in California and she had said that she could start work in six weeks.

"Poor girl," Detective Hudson commented. "She had all that going for her and someone ups and kills her. One thing I have found out though, is that although she didn't use an organised diary system, she did note down people's initials, times and date on tiny little post-it notes and stick them up everywhere. Her work bag is full of them. It will take a while to organise them but that may point to who else was in her life or any appointments she might have had."

"I still favour Peter Riggs for this." Hollis was determined to arrest Riggs for the crime.

Chappell shook his head and said, "Hollis, you saw him. He was practically on the edge of a nervous breakdown. He had turned his back on his best friend and because of that she is dead. It would really have helped us if he could remember who she went to meet and where but since he didn't care he didn't pay any attention. The memory of that will haunt him."

Hollis was adamant. She didn't care if she argued with Chappell in front of the team. "Sir, all I see is someone who is a pretty good actor. You mark my words when we get to the bottom of this Peter Riggs will be there. We've been told that he was seen wandering around her room when she wasn't there, touching her things sitting on her bed. That is definitely obsessive. Jack Danvers said he moved out because, amongst other things, Peter had turned into a creep guy. I think we have to hold him as a firm suspect."

As Hollis spoke Chappell massaged his temples and exhaled loudly. He stared at her. Two bright spots coloured his cheeks while the colour drained from the rest of his face.

Hollis stopped speaking, as she became aware that Chappell was staring at her with fury etched on his face and her colleagues were looking at her in horror.

Chappell let the silence continue for a few seconds before saying, "Need I remind you all and especially you Detective Sergeant Hollis, we operate on evidence. I've said that once already today.

"I want everyone to retrace their steps, do a deeper canvas of the area around Forge Tarn and the lake. I think that we need to look at the character of Jennifer Lindsay more closely. Various people have said that she is an inveterate flirt. We need to look at the implications of that.

"Hollis, get in touch with Marie, Jennifer's friend and question her about that. Find out who Jennifer was seeing, who she was flirting with and who if anyone she was annoying. Did Jennifer go on a date where one thing led to another and she ended up dying?"

Chappell paused, looked at a handful of notes and said, "Jennifer herself complained that she was being pestered by people so, it could be someone we know nothing about at the moment. Lee can you get started on organising those notes with the dates and initials and see how far you get with them. Just remember she knew her killer."

The police officers looked at their desks and began sifting through the information they had so far collected.

"Hollis, a word. In my office. Now."

Chappell stalked through the incident room back to his office. He threw his notes on the desk, stood behind it and crossed his arms.

Hollis got up from her seat and followed him. Hudson whispered "Good luck Hollis" as she passed him.

"Close the door." Chappell barked as soon as Hollis entered. His voice was cold and his face devoid of any emotion.

"Hollis, what do you think you were doing out there? I've already told you that I want evidence not intuition. I don't expect to have to repeat myself to the people in my team. If I have to, then maybe, you aren't ready for the job you have." A muscle in one of Chappell's cheek twitched.

Hollis stood stiffly shuffling from foot to foot. "But sir, I…"

"I haven't finished." Chappell leaned forward and placed his hands on his desk. "Are you ready to be in this team Hollis?" Chappell stared at her. Hollis was silent.

"That was not a rhetorical question. I want an answer. Are you ready to be in this team?"

Hollis bristled, "Yes, yes I am. What I am doing is my job, sir. I am pointing out a person of interest. We may not have any evidence, but we do have the opinion of Jack Danvers."

"Hearsay Hollis. From just one person. You are so fixated on Peter Riggs I want to know why?"

"He reminds me of someone from a case I worked on. A woman accidently killed her boyfriend and pleaded guilty to manslaughter in the end. The victim's best friend had been having an affair with the girlfriend and helped her to cover up the death.

"So, this is just a case of history repeating itself is it? Are you suggesting that Lisa Blaine and Peter Riggs accidently killed Jennifer?"

"No sir, but then again who knows?" Jennifer shrugged and raised her hands. "Sir, I am sorry. I got carried away. Next time I will…"

Chappell interrupted her, "There won't be a next time Hollis. If you have something to say, you will make sure that you have some evidence before you start suspecting people. You certainly won't undermine me in front of my team. Do you understand?"

Hollis nodded. She could feel her eyes watering.

She blinked rapidly and looked at the floor.

Chappell sat down and picked up a sheaf of papers, "Make sure the door doesn't hit you on the way out."

Those members of the team who were still in the incident room pretended to ignore Hollis as she walked back to her desk.

Hudson made no such pretence. He came over to her, "Hey Laura, he's not that bad."

"It's bad enough Lee. It was just so clear that he was having second thoughts about my being here."

Lee chuckled, "When he starts shouting at someone so loudly that you can hear his voice downstairs that's when you need to worry. Did he shout at you?"

"No but.." Hollis slumped over her desk covered her face with her hands and placed her elbows on the table.

"Then don't worry. Well, I mean you should but, he's not going to kick you off the team, not just yet anyway."

Hollis sat up abruptly and looked at Hudson.

"You'll be fine Laura. Chappell's shouted at me a few times and look at me, I'm still here. So is he." Hudson tapped Sampson on the shoulder.

Sampson turned around to face Laura, "Chappell has torn so many strips off me I'm surprised I've got any skin left. Everyone gets shouted at once in a while. If he didn't think you could do it he would have sacked you after the first month. Take on board what he says and just do your best."

Marie chose a vegan coffee bar in which to meet, she was waiting for Hollis when she arrived.

"Marie, hi. I must admit it took me a while to find this place. Is it new?"

Marie nodded, "Aren't you supposed to ask a policeman if you're lost?"

"True but, there wasn't a policeman around."

Marie smiled briefly then her face resumed its grief stricken expression.

Marie said, "Why did she have to die? I don't understand."

Hollis looked apologetic and said, "That's what I'm hoping you can help me with. A few people have said that after splitting up with Lisa, Jennifer's behaviour became unpredictable. They have also said that she flirted with people all the time. Do you know of anyone she was flirting with or beginning to date?"

Marie thought for a few minutes and sipped at her drink. "It's hard to say, I think that Jennifer knew that things were over with Lisa long before she saw Lisa with someone else. Jennifer was always flirting with people even when she was with Lisa. After their break-up, I'd say she went into overdrive. She was just out socialising all the time. She said that she didn't want to stay at home."

Marie paused and said, "I don't think that Jennifer went out looking for people, but she met them in bars, pubs and clubs. She attracted people and they were attracted to her. I know that someone called Rick rang her a few times and she also spoke with Guy. She agreed to meet up with both."

Hollis asked, "How do you know?"

"She took the calls at work. I don't know if she actually met up with them. She'd been fired by then."

"Didn't she talk to you about these things?"

Marie shook her head, "After she'd been fired she

just complained that Mr Southpool kept ringing her up all the time and she was talking about finding a new job."

Hollis said, "Think very carefully. Do remember hearing where she was going to meet up with them?"

Marie answered immediately, "Yes, one in a pub in Bristol and another in a pub at Forge Tarn. That was a few weeks ago, there could have been others. She wanted me to go on a girls' night out. I did once or twice after she was sacked, but she wasn't good company."

Hollis asked, "What do you mean?"

"Her topics of conversation were Mr Southpool, Lisa and how much she could drink before she got drunk. I know that she was miserable, but I wasn't going to sit around and wait for her to pass out through drink."

"When was the last time you spoke with Jennifer?"

"Just a few days ago, she rang me and said that she was thinking of moving to America. I was happy for her, sad for myself but happy for her. Now though, I really have lost a friend."

Hollis asked, "Do you know how things were between her and Peter?"

Marie snorted her disgust and said, "That doormat. Look Peter's a nice person but he just needed to show a bit of backbone. I think that Jennifer liked him well enough. They were schoolfriends, but he seemed to think if he hung around long enough Jennifer would go out with him. He just wasn't her type and he didn't understand that."

Hollis asked, "What was her type?"

"Interesting and passionate. Jennifer wanted to be with someone who had a passion in their lives. Peter is probably the most passionless person you could ever hope to meet.

"I got the impression that they had fallen out. I think that's another reason why she didn't want to stay in at the house on her own with him."

"Thanks Marie, I really appreciate the fact that you've come to talk to me. If you think of anything else please contact me."

Marie nodded, smiled sadly and stood. "Please find out who did this, Detective Hollis. Please."

Chappell sat behind his desk, drinking a glass of water. Hollis had reported back on her interview with Marie and was now giving yet another impassioned appeal as to why she thought Peter Riggs should be brought in for questioning.

"Sir, I know what you said earlier, but now I have two different people saying essentially the same thing about Peter. I know it still isn't hard and fast physical evidence but, I really think that he killed her and if he didn't there's still something that he's not telling us. I cannot believe that he did not know where she was going. You can't help but listen when someone is talking to you. I think he knows. If he does know, why isn't he telling us? And sir, he hasn't exactly been clear about what he did over the weekend."

Hollis paused for breath and watched Chappell consider her suggestion. His brown eyes although looking in her direction were not focused on her. He drank some more water and looked at his picture of the Matterhorn.

"OK, Hollis. Do it. Take Hudson and Sampson and frighten the life out of him. I'll meet you in the interview room when you come back with him. Just make sure you are right about this. I don't want him complaining about police heavy handedness. Are you sure?"

"Yes I am. There's something he's holding back."

The smoke billowed from the corner of the hotel. It rolled in thick clouds over the surrounding area. The first fire engine roared into the car park. The driver executed an emergency stop. The rest of the crew were thrown violently forward.

One of the firemen shouted, "What the hell? The fire's over there, not in the carpark."

The driver replied, "I know but look." He pointed out of the engine's windscreen at the crumpled heap lying directly in his path. On the ground, lay the body of a man. He was unmoving with his limbs sprawled at unnatural angles. The second fire engine stopped behind the first and sounded its alarm. The driver of the first engine left his vehicle and inspected the body. His passengers went to inform the second driver of the problem. With careful manoeuvring the two engines were able to skirt round the corpse and begin to attend to the fire. One of the firemen called the police and informed them of the find.

Peter Riggs shook with fright as he sat in the interview room. Detective Chief Inspector Chappell and Detective Sergeant Hollis sat opposite him. They were grim faced.

Detective Inspector Chappell's eyes drilled into Peter's. Peter started to cry, this time however, neither police officer was sympathetic to his tears. He placed his head in his hands and shook his head.

"No, I didn't kill her. I didn't. You have to believe

me. I didn't do it."

Chappell said, "If you wish us to believe you then you need to tell us the truth. All of the truth not just bits of it. I want to know what you did from last Friday to Monday. You have not told us everything have you?"

"I didn't do it!"

Chappell said, "You are currently the prime suspect in the murder of Jennifer Lindsay. Now is the time to start telling us what you know."

Peter raised his head and looked at the ceiling. "I...I haven't been as truthful as I could have been." Hollis leant forward. Peter continued, "It's just that, well my feelings for Jennifer have been confused for so long.

"I enjoyed being around her. Then she met Lisa and it was obvious that nothing between Jennifer and me would happen. I tried to get on with my own life and go out with my circle of friends, but I was always thinking about what Jennifer was doing. Listening to Jennifer, it became obvious that things with Lisa weren't working out and she was really troubled by it. At night a few times she was so upset that she would crawl into my bed. Nothing happened, she just wanted companionship and someone to talk to."

Peter paused, looked at both police officers and continued, "When we met Lisa and her new girlfriend that night in the restaurant Jennifer went to pieces. She went to the pub and tried to drink herself stupid. I got her back home and put her to bed in her own room. A few hours later there she was in my room, in my bed, wanting to have sex. I turned her down. She got angry and left. She didn't remember a thing the next morning and I didn't bring it up. After that

91

Jennifer would flirt with people and stay out all night. It was worse when she lost her job since she really didn't have any structure to her day. She argued with Jack about using his bike, so she started asking me to drive her about. I was happy to do so. It meant that I could keep an eye on her. I would drop her off, but I wouldn't leave. If she met someone in a coffee shop I would park outside if I could and wait for her. She didn't know. Sometimes she met people and went home with them, I would wait outside. She didn't know that I was there, but I just wanted to check up on her and make sure the she wasn't in trouble."

Peter was silent for a few minutes. Hollis wanted to question him further, but Chappell motioned that she should not speak. At last Peter continued speaking, "Eventually I questioned my motives and wondered if I was becoming a stalker. I cared about her and I could see that she would get herself into trouble. She was drinking a lot and becoming vicious with it. Last week I realised that I had to stop. I just had to cut thoughts of her out of my mind. Last weekend I tried to do that. I went out on Friday with some friends, I can give you their details if you want. On Saturday morning Jennifer shouted at me. She had to get home on her own on Friday and why didn't I come and collect her? I pointed out that I wasn't her taxi service. She calmed down and apologised. She said that she would be going to Forge Tarn on Sunday to meet someone for a date and would I help her out and give her a lift. She said that she wanted to have fun with this particular person. After everything I just said to her there she was asking me to be her chauffer again. I deliberately went out on Saturday and stayed out until Sunday night. I blocked her number and, well, the rest you know. No, I don't know his name or where he lives. All I know is that was where they were supposed to meet."

Hollis asked, "Peter, when you waited outside during the night, can you give a description or the address of these places?"

"No, not really. I would follow her to the house or flat and then drive around the corner. I didn't park right outside their homes. I didn't want Jennifer to catch me. It was dark and I just wanted to catch a glimpse of her leaving."

Hollis was incredulous. She asked, "Peter are you really saying that you waited outside these places and have no idea where they were?"

"It was dark, and I was worried. I didn't take notes of the addresses, just the doors. Can't you see this is what I mean? I killed her. If I had given her the lift she wanted, if I had paid more attention then she'd be alive." Peter glanced hurriedly at his watch.

"Do you have somewhere to be Peter?" Chappell looked at Peter's face and back at his watch.

"No, I just wanted to know what the time was. Look, if you want I could drive around and try and identify the places I think I went to. I don't remember but I could try." Peter shrugged helplessly and wiped his nose on the same grey sweatshirt he had been wearing days earlier.

Chappell ended the interview, "Thank you Peter. It would have been extremely helpful to us if you had told us all of this to begin with."

Back in Chappell's office, Hollis sat feeling deflated.

Chappell said, "Well done, Hollis. You stuck with it. Well done."

"Thank you. But, sir, how can you say, "Well Done"? He did not do it. I've made a fool of myself."

Chappell said, "You stuck with it and you followed your instincts. I'm more convinced that Peter Riggs did not kill Jennifer Lindsay, but he has now given us far more information than he wanted to. His information and his actions point to her state of mind. Her chaotic life style over the past few weeks tends to suggest that she probably annoyed someone, and they snapped. I don't see how the picnic fits in, but we will discover that. Your tenacity is to be commended, don't be so hard on yourself. Now we need…"

He was interrupted by a knock at the door and Dave Sampson's head came into the room.

"Sir, the Twelve Kings Hotel down the road had a fire. It looks like arson. The bar manager, Tom Starkey, has been found dead in the hotel car park. He was found by the firemen; they nearly ran him over. The coroner won't give anything away, but it does look like the man died from manual strangulation. Fortunately, the fire was just in one small corner of the building. It caused a lot of smoke but no real damage, none of the guests or visitors was hurt. They're not doing anything until you get there. They were holding off because you were interviewing a suspect."

Chappell sprang up and dashed out of his office. He ran down the stairs, out of the police station and over to the hotel in a matter of minutes. Hollis had barely made it out of the station, when Chappell slowed down, ran a hand through his hair, straightened his clothes and walked in a professional manner over to the coroner.

"Mike." Chappell nodded

"Hazel."

"Well Mike, most of what I can tell you is that this man has probably been dead for over seven hours and he has bruising around his throat. I'll let you have my report in due course."

"Thanks, Hazel." The coroner walked away and left Mike Chappell to his thoughts.

Two strangulations within a matter of days. What were the odds of that? Chappell looked at the sky and sent up a silent prayer that this body did not represent the beginning of a spate of murders. He turned around at the sound of huffing and puffing. Hollis, Sampson and Hudson were bent over, their hands on their thighs gasping for breath.

Chappell shook his head, "So glad you could make it. It was only a gentle little jog. I thought you all worked out and kept fit."

Hollis looked up, took in Chappell's evil grin, "Yes but you were nought to sixty in one second."

Sampson and Hudson who had yet to regain the power of speech nodded.

"Well team, you are here now. I want to know what caused this fire, who the dead man is and whether or not he is connected with the fire. The coroner tells me that the victim was strangled. I need to know if this is a separate killing or if it is related to that of Jennifer Lindsay. Two strangulations in less than a week cannot be a coincidence."

Chappell strode over to the gurney bearing the dead man and looked at the corpse before he was entirely zipped up in a body bag. Not more than a day earlier this was the man who had served him coffee, and now he was dead. What had this man done to get himself killed? Had he done anything? Had the man finished work and was about to head home or was he having a quick cigarette in the car park? What was the motive for this death?

Back in the incident room, more whiteboards had been wheeled in and this time covered with photographs of the crime scene and of Tom Starkey's body. Chappell inspected each of the photographs that had been stuck up. In some cases, he unpinned the photographs, looked at them closely and put them back up.

He turned and faced his team, "For now, we need to investigate these as two separate deaths. There is nothing for now to suggest that the death of Tom Starkey is connected to the death of Jennifer Lindsay. I think we need to wait for the pathology and forensic reports before we draw conclusions or parallels between these two people.

"Sampson, what did you find out?"

Sampson looked at his notes and said, "Thomas Starkey, Tom for short was thirty-four years old. He was the bar manager and sometimes doubled as the night manager. He had just finished for the night, he was working in the bar, the night manager was elsewhere in the hotel sorting out a customer's problem. The hotel runs a skeleton staff between ten at night and seven in the morning. Tom closed the bar at twelve last night.

"It's hard to tell exactly how many people are registered at the hotel at the moment because the fire has affected the computer systems. It looks like it was an electrical fire that started in a store room. There was no strong smell of accelerants in the vicinity of the store room apart from the cleaning materials already in the room. The fire brigade say that the liquids are toxic and flammable. It seems that there was an adaptor plug which was overloaded and stuck into an extension cable. Due to this the fuse blew or there was a spark which set fire to the materials and the room. Now whether that was deliberate or not remains to be investigated. The cupboard door was opened by a customer service assistant who was looking for an iron. The fire and smoke escaped. She's alright by the way, she was able to raise the alarm."

Chappell addressed Hudson, "What have you found out about Tom Starkey?"

"Thomas Starkey lived on the edge of Bristol in a rented flat. Looking around his lodgings he had qualifications in hospitality and catering and was working his way up to be a hotel manager. At first look there is nothing suspicious about him. He had left a pile of textbooks on his dining room table and a half finished essay on his computer. His bedroom was tidy, all of his clothes were put away and he had a pile of dirty clothes which was already bundled up ready to be taken to a laundry. I think he lived as he worked, his kitchen and bathroom were clean. There does not seem to be anything in his house that would mark him out as a victim. I also looked for signs of a partner, he appears to be single. He has pictures of friends and family dotted around but there was no one in particular. Sampson asked about that at the hotel and his colleagues said that he was single. He had split up with a girlfriend a few years ago. He was driven and ambitious. We won't be able to gain access to his financial records until at least tomorrow."

The rest of the team sat in silence absorbing the information. Chappell turned back to the whiteboards, crossed his arms and stared at the photographs taken from both crime scenes.

"Carry on with both investigations, we are close to solving Jennifer Lindsay's death and we will do the same for Tom Starkey."

The report from the coroner was ready before he left for home.

For a second night that week, Chappell studied the reports from his team and the coroner. Tom Starkey died from strangulation. Chappell studied the pattern of bruising around the throat of the latest murder victim and that of Jennifer Lindsay. The patterns were different. The person who killed Starkey wore gloves, Jennifer's killer did not. Did that mean that Jennifer's death was not premeditated whilst Starkey's was? The weather was quite warm if not wet and foggy, so why would a person wear gloves?

Chappell did not know enough about Tom Starkey to know who might have wanted to kill him. The more Jennifer's death was investigated the more it seemed as if Jennifer had angered someone who lashed out, pushed her, causing her to fall, hit her head and had then been strangled. The trouble with that solution was that it did not explain the staging at the scene. Chappell made a note to ask if Jennifer's blow to the head would have caused her death without having to strangle her.

Reviewing the photographs and reports from both scenes, he made lists of the similarities and the differences. He also made a list of the facts that had yet to come to light. He brewed himself a large cafetière of coffee and worked through the night. He constructed hypotheses, fitted the facts together and thought about those that he would need to know in order to prove his suppositions correct. He continued to do this until he had constructed a list of the information that he needed. When the first rays of a weak sun brightened the sky, Mike Chappell showered, made himself a mug of coffee for the road and set off for work. He called a meeting for seven o'clock.

"Hudson, Sampson and Hollis, I need the following information. Telephone calls made by the victims, the places they frequented, the people they dated, their bank details, where they bought their groceries, which buses they caught, where they spent their spare time. Every inch of their lives will be put under a microscope. I'd also like to know why we haven't had Jennifer's phone records. Get onto it. We need to know. I do not think that Peter and Elle have told us everything they know. Light a fire under them. Make sure they understand that they are in the frame for Jennifer's murder. Speak to Tom Starkey's colleagues again, who was he, why did he want to be a hotelier? Divide the rest of the team between you and make sure that when we meet later today you have most of the answers. The more I think about it, I want you to treat these two murders as if they are connected in some way. I believe that two strangulations in a matter of days is not a coincidence. Either we come across the killer through finding the reason behind Tom Starkey's death or through investigating Jennifer's. Please bear in mind though, that I could be wrong to link these murders, but your investigations will provide the answers. There is a lot of ground to be covered today."

Chappell reserved one task for himself; investigating why Frederick Southpool was connected to both deaths. Jennifer Lindsay was found by Southpool on his land. Southpool was staying in the Twelve Kings Hotel when Tom Starkey was killed. Did Southpool have anything to do with the fire? Why was the computer server damaged? When was the last time there was a fire at the hotel? Mike was running on caffeine and adrenaline, just the way he liked it. He walked over to the hotel and was gratified to see a number of his team interviewing guests and staff.

Hollis was interviewing the hotel's General Manager. Chappell let himself into the manager's room unannounced, both Hollis and the manager Leah Bourdon turned to face him.

Hollis introduced him, "Ms Bourdon, this is Detective Chief Inspector Chappell. Sir, this is Ms Leah Bourdon, the hotel General Manager." Both nodded to each other, Chappell took a seat.

Chappell said, "Forgive me if Detective Sergeant Hollis has already asked you this question, but when was the last time there was a fire at the hotel?"

Ms Bourdon nodded and said, "In fact, she just did. I was about to answer. The last fire we had here that needed the fire crews was over twenty years ago. The hotel was a wreck. It had to be gutted and a major rebuilding programme took place. We've had little fires since, in the kitchen normally, but even so we've only had three of those in the past few years since I've been here."

Chappell smiled at her wanting her to expand on

her answer, "And how long has that been?"

"Six years. I came as an assistant manager and became General Manager two years ago. Nothing like this has happened before. I just hope it doesn't affect the reputation of the hotel." Leah Bourdon, paused, her cheeks paled, "I'm sorry, what with Tom's death that sounds terrible. I didn't mean to sound uncaring."

Chappell asked, "Whose decision was it for the computer back-up system to be located in that storeroom?"

"Mine or Tom's. We just needed it to be somewhere out of the way. The storeroom seemed like the obvious place. It was cool and apart from spare cleaning materials there was nothing else in there."

Hollis asked, "Is there anything that you can tell us about Tom Starkey? What did he do outside of work?"

Leah Bourdon replied, "No, not really. Tom kept himself to himself. He was keen to do well in his job and to learn about all aspects of the role. He had really mastered the new computer system that we had put in. I think that we are going to have to go back to the previous version of it because I really don't know what he used to do. It was a brilliant system though."

Hollis asked, "Why was it so good?"

"Well, not only did it take all the automated bookings, but it logged the drinks and the extra services that guests required with no more than a touch of a button. Then at the end of the stay, we were able to provide guests with detailed bills. Our previous system was not as thorough as the new one."

Chappell asked, "Was Tom the only one able to use it?"

"Oh no, everyone could use it but there are some sections that only managers can access. I must admit that I have so much to do that I let him deal with things such as the payments and refunds. Tom is...I mean was so charming and good with the guests. Some would complain that they had been overcharged and Tom would step in, speak with the angry person and they would leave completely reassured that the bill was correct. I must admit that in the past month or so there were quite a few customers saying that their bills were wrong. With a calm voice and a few key strokes, the money was refunded to their accounts and all was well. He was a great help, I can tell you."

Chappell asked, "Are these refunds automatically returned to the customers' accounts?"

"Yes, yes, I believe they are. Like I said there have been a few problems in the past month. Someone from the IT department was going to have a look at the system and carry out an audit. Now, I guess they will be giving us a completely new system." She hunched her shoulders and drummed her fingers on her thighs.

Hollis asked, "Is there anything else that you can tell us?"

Leah Bourdon shook her head, "I really do not know what he did outside of work. Whilst he was here he showed a lot of initiative. He would make a point of going to the guests' rooms with towels and chocolates. Tom made sure that their rooms were perfect. He definitely helped to set the high level of service I want us to offer and maintain."

Chappell asked, "I was wondering if you knew if your guest Mr Southpool was still here. I would like to talk to him."

"Oh, I'm sorry. He left this morning." Leah Bourdon rose to her feet. "You must excuse me; I really have to get on."

Chappell asked, "Did Mr Southpool say where he was going?"

"I think that he was going home and then he was going travelling. With everything that has been going on, I must admit that I did not give him my full attention. I am sorry, but if there are no other questions, I must attend to a few things."

On the walk back to the police station, Chappell rang Detective Constable Hudson and asked him to chase up Tom Starkey's financial records. He stopped at a coffee shop close to the police station and asked Hollis to join him. It acted as an outpost of the police station. The owner of the shop was a retired policeman who had decorated the coffee shop with memorabilia and pictures from the Keystone Cops television series and was called 'Keystone'.

Most of the patrons were officers taking a break. Chappell urged Hollis to take a seat and queued up to buy their drinks.

"There you go Hollis." Chappell looked around, recognising staff from the police station. He looked at the pictures and memorabilia. He remarked, "The Keystone Cops were a bunch of inept and incompetent policemen. I always wonder if Roy, the owner is having a little joke with us. I certainly feel like one of those cops." He sipped his drink," How's your coffee?"

"Fine, thank you sir. What was it that you wanted to discuss, sir?"

"I have a theory. Based on the evidence or lack of evidence that we have, I think that either one person killed both Jennifer and Tom, or it was a pair of people. The likelihood of two deaths by strangulation being a coincidence would have astronomical odds. We still need to figure out why. I'd like to know how Tom Starkey could afford to live where he did. I also find it strange that there was a higher than average spate of overcharged customers. I think that Ms Bourdon delegated a lot of her job to Tom Starkey. What if he was able to speak to the customers, apply some pressure and they caved in. Instead of the overcharged amounts being refunded to the customer, what if Starkey redirected the money to himself? Does that sound feasible? It is a theory for which I believe evidence will be forthcoming shortly. I may be building castles in the sky but there must have been a lot overcharged customers if Ms Bourdon felt the need to tell us. I wonder if Mr Southpool has anything to do with this?"

"Frederick Southpool? But what does he have to do with this? He found a dead person that he knew on his land. He moved out for a few days just to get away from everything. What with the fire at the hotel he probably decided that it was time to move back home? We've nearly finished at the lake and let's face it his house is not close to the lake."

"That's my point. Two deaths by strangulation, days and miles apart. How is it that Frederick Southpool is present or at least in the vicinity of both?"

"Just unlucky, I guess."

"Hollis, think." Chappell gave her a sharp disapproving look. "I know that behind all of this you want Peter Riggs to be Jennifer Lindsay's killer, he may yet be, but I doubt it. Open your mind and review the facts as they are."

Hollis lowered her head and gazed into her drink. "I'm sorry, sir. You are right, I guess that I am locked into that idea."

"Yes, well you need to be flexible. There's nothing wrong with having a hunch but you need to change your mind as new facts come to you. And, you definitely need evidence if you plan on arresting someone."

Hollis said, "What I would ask though, is what motive does Frederick Southpool have to kill Jennifer?" Hollis took a sip from her drink and gave Chappell an appraising look over the top of her coffee cup. "Sir, Frederick Southpool should want her to stay alive especially if he wanted her to help him. Alright, he lost his temper with her but he's not going to want to kill her if he thinks that she can help him."

"That is the question, what does Southpool have to do with these deaths? To get the answer to that we are going to do one thing, I've made appointments to see Samuel Adesinsi later. At the end of the day Hollis, I'm playing a hunch too. I could be wrong."

"Sir, I still want to stick with Peter Riggs." Hollis held a hand up, "Please, listen." Chappell who had been about to speak nodded and drank his coffee.

"Go ahead Hollis. I won't interrupt you."

"I think that if Peter Riggs did not kill Jennifer, I bet he knows who did. There is something he is not saying. I just can't believe that he could wait outside a house and not know the area he was in. If he followed a bus home he should have been able to give us the number of it." Hollis' face glowed with enthusiasm as she warmed to her topic.

"Hollis, if you feel so strongly about this perhaps you should do something. Do you think that you can get anything else from him?" Chappell looked doubtful but said nothing else.

"I don't want to pull him in again. I want to watch him. I wonder if he will return to the places that he waited for Jennifer. If he does, we might be able to catch someone out."

"What, all day? We don't have the manpower for that."

"No, I'll follow him, and I'll do it at night. If that is alright?" Hollis shifted in her chair, leant forward and continued, "I don't know if you noticed but when we questioned him about waiting outside the properties at night, I just got the impression that there was one last thing he hadn't told us."

Chappell narrowed his eyes and looked towards the ceiling. He thought about Hollis' suggestion, blew out a breath and nodded.

He said, "Yes do it Hollis. We've got nothing to lose. There is not a lot for us to go on at this point. Do it. Hudson and Sampson can work on the Starkey murder. Yes, do it Hollis."

Chappell stood, drained his mug and placed it back on the table. He nodded to Hollis and strode out of the coffee shop. Hollis sat at the table staring into space planning her next move. She looked at her watch. It was afternoon. She had no idea of Peter Riggs' daily routine. Where to start? What did she know about Peter Riggs?

Peter Riggs was a trainee psychologist. He was

undertaking a work placement with a clinic. She would drive over to his lodgings and wait for him to return home. It was a long shot, but she wanted to know if she could learn anything else about him by carrying out some surveillance.

Scaffolding had been erected at the front entrance of Southpool Computing. The windows were being cleaned and a new sign was being hung. Mike Chappell dodged around the cleaners and made his way to the reception desk. Samuel Adesinsi who was speaking with a receptionist looked up when he saw Chappell.

"Detective Chief Inspector Chappell. Hello again. Please follow me."

Once again Samuel led the way to the boardroom, opening the door, he said, "Please take a seat, I just have to finish talking to the receptionist." Samuel left swiftly.

Chappell entered the room and glanced around. The pictures of Frederick Southpool and his son Robert were still stacked against a wall. Chappell crouched down and combed through the photographs once again. He covered his mouth with a hand. An idea was forming in his mind. No, it couldn't be. Could it? But why? What was the motive? Chappell ran his hand over his face as if washing it. Had he just stumbled on the 'how' of the murder of Jennifer Lindsay? He did not trust himself to consider the idea any further.

Samuel Adesinsi returned. He looked enquiringly at Chappell, "Detective Chief Inspector are you feeling alright? You look as if you have seen a ghost."

"A ghost of an idea, perhaps. Mr Adesini, please

do not remove these pictures from this room. They are very important and must be kept."

"Yes, certainly. As you wish."

"Mr Adesini, I have to leave now. In fact, I think I have the information that I need. Thank you for your help."

"But I haven't done anything."

"You have. More than you will ever know. Thank you." Chappell turned to leave, "Oh, does Frederick Southpool have permission to use the company account at the Twelve Kings Hotel?"

"Yes, he does. Anything to keep him from setting foot on the premises. We need to sort that out actually."

"Why?"

"Frederick doesn't actually own any property. The farm, his house, the properties in town they are all owned by the company. When the business became a limited company, he was able to say that he did not own anything. However, now that he has lost control of the business he either needs to buy the property back or walk away."

Chappell nodded, "So it was effectively a dodge then?"

"You could say so." Samuel spread his hands, palms up and shrugged.

"Samuel, can you send the information about the properties, Frederick Southpool does, or rather does not own to me. I would be very interested to see."

"Is Frederick under investigation?"

"Not at the moment. Please just send the information. I would appreciate it very much if you could do so as speedily as possible."

"Of course. I will make sure that it is emailed to

you by the end of the day."

Chappell ran from the building, out to his car and tore out of the car park. He gunned his car in the direction of Forge Tarn. He had to visit the lake again. Parts of the jigsaw puzzle were beginning to take shape. He had a thread that he could pull on and unravel the mystery at last. Raindrops spattered the car windscreen. The dark gloomy clouds which had hung threateningly above for the last few days, shed their load. Within seconds the rain fell so heavily that Chappell's visibility was reduced to just a few feet ahead of him. The rain was torrential. Deep puddles formed on the road. Pedestrians had been caught unaware. Some were already drenched. People were scurrying for cover in shops and doorways. Chappell continued to drive as quickly and as carefully as he could. There was something that he needed to see at the crime scene. With the rain lashing down it was now doubtful that it was preserved but he had to see for himself.

Chappell parked in the car park at the far end of the lake and ran along its perimeter, choosing the side where the rotted rowing boat was chained up. He did not stop to look at it but instead ran further still to the crime scene itself. He ducked under the police tape and stared about him. The rain had created rivulets in the mud. There was nothing to show that a murder had been committed and a body found. Chappell was disappointed that he could not find what he had wanted to see. He was certain that a picture of it existed when SOCA had photographed the area. He hoped and prayed that this was the case. Mike Chappell stood exactly where the picnic had once been laid out and looked towards the other end of the lake. He smiled. Yes, this was definitely how the body of Jennifer Lindsay had ended up at this end of the lake. Where she had been killed was another matter. He had made progress of a kind. Now to follow the thread wherever it took him.

Hollis was parked around the corner from the lodging house. She had seen Elle Latimer return and let herself into the house. There was no sign of Peter. Hollis had researched the type of car and the number plate of the car that he drove. It was a blue, seven-year-old Fiat 500. This was parked directly outside the house. Hollis had no way of knowing if he was at home, but she would take the chance and believe that Peter Riggs had yet to return.

She had been parked outside the house for two hours already. She was prepared to wait the whole night through, if it would help her to find out more about her chief suspect. He arrived home an hour later. Peter was carrying a bag of groceries. Before he could open the door, Elle Latimer opened it from her side and stepped out. Peter and Elle had a short conversation. Hollis was not close enough to overhear what was being said. Elle was carrying a large black holdall and a handbag. Elle scanned the road as if looking for someone. Hollis slid down behind the wheel in her car. It was unlikely that Elle could see her, but if Hollis could see Elle anything was possible. A few moments later, a sleek navy blue saloon car drew up beside Elle. With a wave to Peter, Elle walked over to the car, opened the front passenger door and slid in. The door had barely closed before the car pulled off. Peter stood outside the house and looked at the car as it disappeared into the distance. At last, he walked into the house and closed the door.

Hollis sat in her car waiting for Peter Riggs to come out again. He did not. She watched the house as lights went on and went off. She saw heavy drapes being drawn across the windows. The hallway light, which could be seen through the glass window at the top of the front door, went off at eleven o'clock. As far as Hollis could tell the house was in darkness, from the front at least. She waited until three o'clock and decided to go home. Hollis knew that she was not wrong. One night very soon, Peter Riggs would retrace the drive he took when he dropped off Jennifer and when he did, she would be waiting for him. It was an instinct, but she was sure he would do it.

Tom Starkey's financial information was sent through to the detectives. Hudson and Sampson visited Chappell in his office.

Hudson spoke first, "Sir, you're not going to believe this"

"Try me."

"Well sir, I ran the dead man's fingerprints. It turns out that Thomas Starkey is a Swiss national called Thomaz Strenzi. He was a hotel employee who demanded money with menaces. He's wanted for assault and for actual bodily harm. He absconded from the hotel where he worked with the weekly takings. Let's see," Hudson flicked through his notes. "Yes, he absconded with the equivalent of £50,000 right after some fancy ball. He had programmed the hotel's computer to pay some of the money into his account and he took some cash and paid that in over the counter."

Sampson handed Chappell the financial documents he had been holding. "Read through that sir, what do you see? That's his current account."

Chappell did as asked and commented, "I see payments for his rent and utilities and nothing else. He has not made a single withdrawal. So, what is he living on?"

Hudson and Sampson smiled broadly at Chappell as he spoke his thoughts out aloud. "Tom Starkey, let's call him that, has a Swiss bank account. He pulls the same trick over here that he pulled in Switzerland. He diverts money to his account, an account which no one knew about. I wonder if he demanded money with menaces over here too."

Sampson commented, "I bet Starkey set the fire at the hotel as soon as he heard that an audit was going to be carried out."

Chappell said, "Very definitely. Good work you two. The computer system might have been destroyed but I wonder if he destroyed the central records. See if you find evidence of money from the hotel being diverted to a Swiss account. I have a feeling that he may have been blackmailing guests, overcharging them and paying the extra money into this account. We just need to find out who took exception to his scheme and killed him."

Chappell had spent the previous night poring over the photographs from the crime scene. More than ever, he was certain that he knew how Jennifer's body could have been placed in the lake. He had suspicions about Frederick Southpool but why would he have killed her?

Mike turned from looking at the whiteboards and faced Hollis as she entered the incident room. She looked tired and deflated.

"No joy, Hollis?"

"No sir, afraid not?"

"Stick with it. This is your hunch, play it and see where it takes you."

Hollis looked doubtful. She threw herself into her chair and surveyed the mountain of paperwork that had accumulated on her desk.

Chappell called out to the other members of his team, "Hudson, Sampson, what have you found out about Starkey's movements?"

Sampson spoke up, "Starkey seems to have just gone to work and then gone home. His neighbours barely saw him. When they did, he normally arrived home when they left for work. His phone has hardly been used. He probably made any phone calls he needed to from work."

Chappell nodded and said, "So on the surface we have two unrelated deaths. They appear motiveless because we don't know what motivated the killer or killers to commit the crimes. We are closer to find a motive for Thomas Starkey's death than Jennifer's. I want you to start to concentrate your efforts on Frederick Southpool. He was at the Twelve Kings and Jennifer's corpse was found on his land. I don't know why these murders were committed but I feel that Southpool will be connected."

Hollis started to speak "But sir, what about..."

Chappell interrupted her, "Stick with Riggs, Hollis. I am not discounting anything or anyone. If you are right about Peter Riggs he may well lead us to some further valuable information. At this stage, I wonder if he might turn into a vigilante and solve the murder for us." Chappell grimaced whilst the rest of the team grinned.

It was rare for Chappell to indulge in humour, dark or otherwise. It was a sign of the desperate state of the case.

Chappell continued, "Seriously though, I think that we are in the end game. If the murders are connected the killer will want to get away. Again, I point to Southpool deciding to go home and then to go travelling. Why would he do that when he is trying to set up a new company to market his new, as yet unwritten program? He checked out of the hotel after the death of Starkey. Could Southpool have said or done something that Starkey was blackmailing him about? Now there is something else I want to bring to your attention."

Chappell walked back to the whiteboard and pulled a photograph of the crime scene where Jennifer was found from it. He passed it around the team. "What do you see?"

Hudson answered first, "The crime scene which we know is staged." Sampson and Hollis nodded.

"Have another look?"

Each of the detectives pored over the photograph in turn. Hollis said, "What should we be looking at sir?"

"When you see it, you will not be able to miss it. Have one more look."

Hollis, Hudson and Sampson tried but failed to find anything. All that they saw was a picnic set out on the grass. The mud beside the lake had a few indentations but no footprints. A fact which had caused the initial mystery of how the body appeared beside the lake. There were no footprints anywhere.

Chappell walked into his office and came back with a larger blow-up of the photograph he had passed around.

Hollis gave an exasperated sigh, "Sir, can you just tell us?"

Chappell held up the large photograph, "Those indentations you can see are footprints." He pointed to the prints in the mud of the picture he was holding. "They are the footprints of a person wearing flippers." The team gazed at the smaller picture and then the larger version.

Chappell continued, "I've looked at the picture so often and then I looked at the pictures back at Southpool Computing. Southpool can scuba dive. What if he somehow used his equipment to deposit the body of Jennifer Lindsay on the far side of the lake. He wouldn't be seen. He could also take the food in a waterproof bag and lay it out on the bank."

His team greeted his suggestion with silence.

Chappell felt the need to justify himself, "I know it sounds farfetched, but it is the only option that fits the facts. A woman's body is found beside a lake with no footprints at the scene. Food is laid out for a picnic which she does not eat. Nobody sees her there and more importantly there is no evidence apart from the footprints made by the flippers."

"So, sir, why am I following Peter Riggs?"

"I think that Riggs may have some part to play. I believe that there may be an accomplice. I have no evidence for this just a feeling. The murders, although similar are different. Don't forget Jennifer was killed by someone using their bare hands. The coroner tells me that the blow to the back of the head may have rendered Jennifer Lindsay unconscious, but it would not have killed her. Tom Starkey was killed by someone wearing gloves. In this weather you need an umbrella but not gloves. One murder may have been impulsive and the other premeditated.

Hollis and Hudson, this evening I want you to follow Peter Riggs. You have convinced me that he might try to retrace the route he drove when he followed Jennifer. Hopefully his interview with us has planted a seed. Sampson, Samuel Adesini should be sending over a list of the properties that Southpool 'owns' in and around town. I want to know who lives in them and if there is any personal connection with Southpool. In the meantime, Hollis I want you to accompany me to see Southpool at home. We need to interview him one last time. It may encourage some action on his part."

Frederick Southpool's house was located a mile from the lake. The road from the village of Forge Tarn was dotted with 'private property' signs. Chappell wondered if Southpool would have the money to buy back his property. A narrow road led from the main road to the farmhouse itself. From the outside the house looked in good condition. It was built from pale Cotswold stone and was a two storey building. Hollis who had driven, parked the car next to a gleaming black Mercedes sportscar. She made a point of feeling the bonnet of the car.

"The engine is still warm. Maybe Mr Southpool is at home."

Chappell made to walk to the front door of the house but was challenged by a ferocious chicken who squawked and pecked at his feet. More chickens joined the first and he was soon surrounded. A short, rotund woman left the house and shooed the birds away.

"Can I help you?"

"Yes, I hope so. I am Detective Chief Inspector Chappell, and this is Detective Sergeant Hollis. I wondered is Mr Southpool at home?"

"No, I'm afraid he's not. He left not more than fifteen minutes ago."

"Can I help you? Why don't you come in? I'm sure it's going to rain again."

Much like his business headquarters, the inside of Frederick Southpool's house comprised of mirrored glass and steel. In keeping with his tastes, the wooden floors were of bleached oak. The furniture was of a minimalist design giving the impression that one had walked into a show home. Sculptures and paintings adorned walls, tables, shelves and display plinths. The artworks were undoubtedly expensive but certainly not appealing to Chappell. He wondered if he was in a home or an art gallery.

On one carved wooden plinth were a number of photographs. Some were of Frederick Southpool shaking hands with business dignitaries and others were of Frederick and his son Robert. Here again, were photographs of the pair holidaying in exotic parts of the world. They were dressed in wetsuits and holding harpoons.

Edith Shorely, the housekeeper waddled through the lower floor rooms and took them to the kitchen. The farmhouse was large and rambling. Chappell and Hollis walked past a few rooms as they walked through the house. The kitchen was the warmest and the most welcoming place. There was an Aga range and a large oak table with accompanying chairs.

"Edith what can you tell us about Frederick Southpool?" Chappell smiled encouragingly at her.

Edith bustled about her domain preparing tea and fetching biscuits. She seemed to like the attention.

Once seated, she was ready to regale the police officers with everything she knew about Frederick Southpool. She touched on his loss of the company and the finding of Jennifer's body.

Hollis asked, "Edith do you have any idea why Mr Southpool would want to live out here?"

"Well, I think it's because he liked the idea of being a farmer. It massaged his ego. I remember he went to the shops and bought a lot of what he called his farming clothes. Sometimes he would say, "Edith, I'm a farmer" then he would laugh. I think really, he was looking for a big house in the area and this came up. Dave, the farmer who sold it to him, had made quite a bit of money from the sale."

"Does he take any interest in the farm?"

"No not really. There is a tenant farmer, Phil, living in one of the smaller houses not far away. Phil runs the farm, Frederick Southpool just owns it."

"What is life like here in this house?"

"Well Robert, Mr Southpool's son, has his own place in town so it is really just Mr Southpool and me. I make sure that the meals are cooked, the laundry is done, and I vacuum and dust. He's not here enough to make a mess. To be honest with you, I don't like this place much. It leaves me cold."

Chappell asked, "Is Mr Southpool divorced or widowed?"

"He's divorced. A long time ago. I've been

working here for eight years and I know that he was divorced before then."

Hollis asked, "Did you know Jennifer Lindsay, the young woman who died by the lake?"

"Oh yes, I did. That was absolutely dreadful. I really liked her. She was helping Mr Southpool with a special project of his. Something happened, I don't know what and then she was sacked from the company. Is that right? I can't think what she could have done, Mr Southpool really depended on her. Do you know what happened?"

Keen to keep Edith on the topic, Chappell asked, "Were you here when Mr Southpool found Jennifer?"

"No, no I wasn't. That was Sunday wasn't it? I don't live here. I live in the village. Mr Southpool had said that he might not be staying here and that he might just stay at the Twelve Kings, so he gave me the weekend off."

Hollis doubled checked, "So, you don't know for certain if he was actually here on Sunday?"

"Well not for certain but, I'm sure that he would probably have been here over the weekend. It's not like he would have any business meetings. He does like to go for a jog around the grounds on a Sunday morning. He said it clears his head."

"Edith, does Mr Southpool have his own scuba diving equipment? I've noticed quite a few pictures of him in wet suits."

"Yes, he does."

"Can we have a look at it?"

Edith looked at him warily, "I'm not sure. Are you here to search the house? Don't you need a warrant for that?"

Chappell gave an easy disarming smile, "No, I

don't want to conduct a search. I just wondered if you would be able to tell me if Mr Southpool possesses scuba diving equipment and if he does, where might it be kept? That's just a question, I don't want to look in any dark corners. Would you be able to answer that question for me?"

"Well, yes he does. Normally it would be in the shed out the back by the chicken coop. Just before you came I saw him putting luggage into his Range Rover. I don't know if he packed the equipment. He told me that he was about to go on holiday."

Chappell asked, "Do you know where he was going?"

"He was going to collect his son, Robert and then they were going travelling. That's all he said to me. I'm really sorry I can't be any more helpful."

"No, that is alright Edith. I think that you have been very helpful. Would you mind going into the shed and having a look for the equipment?"

The housekeeper looked doubtfully at Hollis, who in return gave her a beaming smile. Edith struggled to her feet and gazed at the two police officers.

"I'll go and have a look. You two stay here though. Don't move a muscle."

"We won't," Chappell replied.

A few moments later, Edith returned, ashen faced and slumped into a chair. Her mouth opened and closed a few times before she was able to make a sound.

"There's blood in there. There's blood in the shed."

Chappell said, "Show me."

Chappell was on his feet and striding out of the

kitchen in the direction of the shed. Hollis helped Edith to her feet and allowed the woman to lean on her as they walked at a slower pace. By the time they reached the large, wooden shed, Chappell was looking into the dim interior of the building. A range of gardening and D-I-Y tools were arranged either on the floor or hanging from hooks attached to the rafters or walls. Leaning against one wall beside the doorway was a metal spade. It was resting on its handle while the blade was uppermost. On the edge of the blade was congealed blood. On closer inspection hairs were trapped in the mess of blood. On the ground beside the spade was a large dirty rag. This too, was covered in blood. It appeared to have been used to clean the spade. Instead, whoever had attempted to clean the spade had smeared the blood over the tool.

Hollis commented, "That's a lot of blood."

"That wound on the back of Jennifer's head was substantial and it probably led to her being rendered unconscious."

The officers had forgotten about the presence of Edith. The housekeeper whimpered, more frightened of the conversation taking place than at the evidence of a crime.

"Hollis, you take Edith back to the house. I'll ring SOCA. I want this area sealed off. This could be the primary crime scene. We need to find Frederick Southpool. He is now our chief suspect."

The processing of the scene was expedited as quickly as possible, as was the issuing of a search warrant. Chappell sat behind his desk, studying photographs of the scene at the lake and of the inside the shed. There was no doubt in his mind that Frederick Southpool was guilty of Jennifer's murder. He thought about how it might have happened. Both Jennifer and Southpool had had violent outbursts over the past few weeks. Had Southpool managed to lure Jennifer to his home? Southpool would have needed Jennifer's expertise if he was to set up a new company. She may have agreed to visit. Once with him, their conversation descended into a violent argument and he strangled her? As she fell she hit her head causing her to bleed. Perhaps he had worn his wetsuit and transported her body underwater to the other side of the lake. The circumstantial evidence against Southpool was mounting up. Chappell was sure that Southpool was probably also guilty of killing Tom Starkey, but as of yet there was not a shred of evidence to prove this supposition. There were a few pieces of the puzzle missing and Chappell did not know what they were or where to look for them.

A knock at the open office door was followed by Dave Sampson stepping into the room.

"Sir, Southpool's vehicle has not been seen. We've been looking at traffic cameras, but we can't find it on any major roads. We've had a look at the three properties he has. The apartments are located within two tower blocks. He has two properties in the same block. All apartments have been let. The trouble is the two blocks are located in town and have underground parking. There were no maintenance people or security guards when we called. We've rung the property management agents and they are sending people over to meet us, after they find their keys.

Sir, I'm just popping downstairs to get a drink. Can I get you one?"

"Yes please. I'll pay for both."

Chappell reached into his jacket pocket and withdrew a bundle of receipts and some crumpled ten pound notes. He laid the receipts on his desk and handed two ten pound notes to Sampson.

"Buy the drinks and food for the team from this." Sampson advanced and took the money. He glanced down at the receipts on the desk.

"Mind you sir, that's a lot of coffee you've been drinking." The coffee shop's logo was clearly visible of the receipts.

"Coffee makes the world go 'round Dave." Sampson nodded and left.

As a way to momentarily distract himself, Chappell smoothed out the receipts and looked at how much coffee he had actually drunk over the past few days. He looked at how many times a day he had bought the coffee. He stopped. He sped outside and looked at the evidence boards laden with photographs.

"No, no it can't be, can it?" Chappell muttered to himself as he searched for a particular series of pictures. Ideas were coming thick and fast to him, he needed time to process what he had just realised.

"Hollis, Hudson, drop what you are doing. Hudson go downstairs and find officer Barnes. If he's not on duty, find him and drag him in here if you have to. Hollis where are your notes from when we interviewed Southpool at the hotel? Find them. Both of you get going now."

Chappell found the photograph he was looking for. At the supposed picnic he remembered that some food had been laid out on a slip of paper. The piece of paper had been a receipt. Hollis found her notes, Hudson came back accompanied by a somewhat flustered Officer Barnes whilst Sampson came back laden with drinks and pastries.

Chappell paced up and down the incident room, "Toby, can you remind me again when Frederick Southpool came to make his report."

"Well sir, he came in about three o'clock in the afternoon and just waited. I didn't speak to him until forty minutes later. He just sat and waited and then told me about the drowning."

"You're sure he was there at three and you didn't speak to him until three-forty?"

"Yes sir. There are cameras and I wrote the time and date down when he spoke to me."

"Good man. Thank you Toby. Well done. You can go."

Toby Barnes left the room hurriedly he had no desire to be questioned by Detective Chief Inspector Chappell again. Being pulled up the stairs by Detective Sergeant Hudson was bad enough.

Chappell looked at his team, "You just heard him. Southpool came in at three and didn't make his report until three-forty. My question is why was the food laid out for the picnic accompanied by a receipt that was printed at three-twenty?" Chappell waved the picture of the receipt around before handing it to the team.

Hollis exclaimed, "That means that Southpool was not acting alone. He had an accomplice. He comes here to make the report and the accomplice buys the food and sets the scene. This isn't about anyone caring enough about Jennifer to make it seem like she was having a picnic. This is about giving Frederick Southpool an alibi."

"Yes Hollis. Read your notes, what did Southpool say about his whereabouts on Sunday?"

Hollis flicked through her notebook.

"Southpool said that he was at home on Sunday, went for a jog and put himself through a punishing schedule. He moved back to the hotel after Jennifer's death."

Chappell grinned, "And then what happened?"

"Nothing sir, nothing."

"No Hollis. Something did. What happened was the barman dropped a glass. That barman was Tom Starkey. Starkey had just heard Southpool give us a barefaced lie and he dropped the glass. He probably couldn't believe what he had heard. I suspect that Starkey confronted Southpool about it and was killed.

"What I think is that Southpool wasn't at home at all. He had given Edith the weekend off and had stayed at the hotel. What if his accomplice, and at this stage I am willing to bet that it was his son, was the one who killed Jennifer? What if the son kills Jennifer, rings his father and his father tells him what to do? That's why Southpool is in no hurry to make his report. He has to wait until his son Robert has set the scene. That's also why he gave the reason that he acted on automatic and drove over here to the police station instead of ringing us."

Hollis, Hudson and Sampson nodded in agreement.

Chappell stopped his pacing, "So this is what I want done, notify the airports about Frederick and Robert Southpool. Go and check on the properties. I bet that the vehicle was left in one of the underground carparks while the Southpools took a taxi to the airport."

Hollis asked, "Why an airport? They could have driven straight to London or anywhere, Wales or just kept going up to Scotland."

"With two murders under their belts, I think that they would want to leave the country as soon as possible. Hollis don't bother with following Peter Riggs. Put him in a car and drive him to both the apartment buildings, something might jog his memory. I have a feeling that Jennifer may have had a date with Robert Southpool."

Sampson asked, "One question sir, what were Jennifer and the son doing up at the house?"

Chappell responded, giving as full an answer as he could, "That's a question we can ask later. We know that Jennifer liked going to the lake. It might be that she had met Robert Southpool previously and was happy to accompany him to the house. We already know that she was moody and unpredictable. Something happened, and it was Robert who placed her in the lake.

"I think that this is a case of a father trying to cover up his son's crime and the second death was because he lied in the presence of someone who knew the truth. If Starkey had come to us instead of trying to blackmail Southpool he'd be alive. Notify the airports and check the properties. We should be able to clear this up shortly.

"Frederick Southpool clearly loves his son. That is one of the first things that Samuel Adesini told us. A loving parent would do anything to protect their child." Chappell gave Hollis, Hudson and Samson deep penetrating stares, "Including murder and covering up a murder."

Peter Riggs was waiting outside his lodgings when Hollis drove up beside him. She had already explained the purpose of the exercise during her earlier phone call. Peter had agreed to help.

He opened the front passenger door and slid into the seat.

Hollis said, "Peter I need you to concentrate and think. We have two possible addresses where Jennifer's killer might be. I need you to help me to identify which one is the most likely."

"I'll try. I hope I can do this."

Hollis replied, "Not to worry Peter, just do your best. Let's go to the first address and see if you recognise it."

Both occupants of the car were quiet. Laura Hollis concentrated on driving while Peter looked out for any roads and landmarks that he recognised. Hollis arrived at the first of the properties. The roads were busy, Hollis was forced to drive far slower than she would have liked.

She explained what she wanted Peter to do, "There are two possible properties in this tower block that Jennifer could have visited. Does this area look familiar?"

Peter shook his head, "No not at all. I don't recognise anything."

"Ok Peter, why don't you get out and walk around like you did when you were following Jennifer. Things are going to look different in daylight."

Peter did as suggested and wandered about.

Returning to the car he said, "Detective, I really don't recognise this place." Peter was genuinely disappointed. "There is nothing about this place that I've seen before."

Hollis spoke with more optimism than she felt, "Well there is one other location."

Starting the car, she headed off towards it.

Chappell who was seated at his desk, looked at the pages of information Samuel had sent him. Southpool owned three apartments which had been rented out. Mike could sense that there was something he was missing. In their haste the team had looked only at the apartments that Southpool had once owned. More information had been provided than just naming the three properties. Adesini knew that Chappell had only been interested in the properties once owned by Southpool, so why had he sent so much information?

Chappell tried to put himself in the place of Frederick Southpool. If he were a rich doting father what would he do? Would he let his son rent a flat from him or the company or would he buy a property and give it to his son outright? Chappell would just give his child a deposit towards a property but what would Southpool do? The list of information he was reading showed all the properties that Southpool Computing had owned, bought and sold over the past ten years. Chappell needed to make sense of it. Somewhere buried in this list was the possible location of where the Southpools were hiding.

Hollis was now parked outside the second property. Peter had wandered around the area. There was nothing about this location that he recognised either. There were a few landmarks such as a large modern church on one street corner and a cinema on another.

Peter said, "Detective, I think I would remember if I had sat outside that church or that cinema. No, wherever I was it wasn't here."

Hollis was deflated. She had been so sure that she would be proved correct. Three buses drove past her, stopped at their designated stops and disgorged their passengers. Hollis looked at the number of people who had lined up at the buses.

An idea came to her, "Peter didn't you say that there was a bus route near where Jennifer was? You waited until she caught a bus. Could this be the bus route?"

"Yes," Peter said as he looked out of the windscreen and looked at the buses as they drove further along the road. "This road is on the bus route I followed."

Hollis suggested, "Do you think if we follow the bus route you might recognise something."

Hollis started the car, the three buses, although bearing different destinations, were following each other. She followed the buses. The traffic had built up along the road. There were a series of road works and accompanying temporary traffic lights. The delays were becoming frustrating.

After ten minutes, she asked, "Do you recognise anything yet?"

"No, but this is the bus route I know that for sure. I'm hoping I will recognise the block of flats."

Hollis continued driving. As she did so she asked Peter to describe what he remembered of the last property he followed Jennifer to.

"It's coming back to me now; it was a dark night though. I remember I was parked opposite a kebab shop. Jennifer went into a block of flats that wasn't that modern. It was well-kept though. It probably only had three floors. The flats at the front had large windows. I do remember that. One flat had a really unique lampshade. It wasn't exactly a lampshade, maybe it was more of a chandelier. I remember it was such a big thing that you couldn't miss it. It was like a work of art."

"Well, that is something for us to keep our eyes open for," Hollis said doubtfully. She continued driving. Hollis looked for the kebab shop while Peter looked out for the flat with the chandelier. The pavement was so crowded that Hollis had trouble identifying the type of food outlets they were passing.

After reading through several pages of information Chappell came to a page that was headed, 'Gifts and Loans'. Only one property was listed. The property had been disposed of as a gift to Robert Southpool. This had to be the address and where the Southpools were hiding.

Walking into the incident room Chappell called out to Hudson and Sampson, "I think I know where the Southpools might be. Is Hollis back yet?"

Hudson replied, "No, sir. She rang to say that Peter Riggs hadn't recognised the two properties and now they were following a bus route but that was about ten minutes ago."

Chappell grimaced, "Both of you come with me. Hollis might be lucky and find the Southpools. I'm a little concerned about what will happen if they see her and what might happen if she sees them. Southpool will know who she is." Chappell turned and raced down the stairs to the car park. Hudson and Sampson were at his heels.

Hollis had been driving for twenty minutes and was beginning to feel as if she was on a wild goose chase. Peter was also becoming disheartened. Hollis carried on driving trying to keep their hopes up.

"There, there it is." Peter bounced up and down in his seat. He pointed to the block of flats. Hollis scanned the area. Yes, there was the kebab shop and opposite that was the block of flats. With no curtains covering the window, a huge unlit chandelier could clearly be seen in one of the front windows. Hollis stopped abruptly. The driver behind her honked his horn in rebuke. Hollis pulled over to the kerb.

"Looks like you've done it Peter." Hollis smiled at him. She sat staring at the building. She looked around. In addition to the kebab shop there was a coffee shop and a pub. Either would make an ideal vantage point for her to start her surveillance.

Hollis said, "Thank you Peter. This is great. I need to stay here. Will it be alright if you take the bus back home?"

"That's fine. In fact, there's a bus coming now." Peter was out of the car and running towards the nearest bus stop before Hollis had a chance to say goodbye to him. Hollis had no way of knowing where the Southpools were, or even if they could see her. She had to work on the assumption that they were not expecting to be found and would not be looking out for the police. She sat in the car for a few minutes longer. Even if the Southpools were looking out for her, there were such a large mass of people she might easily be overlooked.

Frederick Southpool had indeed spotted the car parked opposite the block of flats. His flat was the one which possessed the elaborate chandelier. He had been peering periodically out of the front window as he waited for his son to pack a few items and find his passport. He had kept a note of any vehicle which parked close by and did not move off soon after. The driver of the navy blue car was just sitting in it. Southpool kept to one side of the large bay window and looked down on Hollis' car. The angle of the sunlight was such that he had no difficulty in identifying the driver. Detective Sergeant Hollis was a striking looking woman. With her shoulder length curly hair, she was easily recognisable. Southpool looked up and down the road, making sure to keep behind the long drapes covering the window. He had no way of knowing if the police woman was on her own. Damn. How had the police tracked him down so quickly? He thought that he would have had enough time to make it to an airport. He walked away to find his son and to decide what to do.

Hollis looked longingly at the coffee shop. She definitely needed a drink and a break from driving. Stepping out of the car, intending to walk towards the coffee shop, she debated whether or not to ring in her location. Deciding to ring the team when settled in the coffee shop, she rolled her shoulders trying to ease her cramped muscles. A breeze ruffled her hair and blew it against her face. Pulling a hair band from her wrist she gathered her hair into a ponytail.

As she bent to retrieve her handbag from the car, she was aware that there was a man standing close to her on either side. A hand was placed on each of her arms above the elbow.

"Detective Sergeant Hollis, keep walking and don't make a sound. If you do, I'll break your arm." Hollis turned towards the speaker. It was Frederick Southpool. On the other side of her was his son Robert. She was being led along the street away from the block of flats. Her fellow pedestrians thought nothing of the three people walking abreast and taking up the pavement. The Southpools did not for one moment let go of her arms.

The change in Robert was striking. When she had seen him at the hotel he had looked presentable. Now, his hair was greasy and sticking to his forehead, he was pale and unshaven. He appeared to be wearing the same clothes she had seen him in before.

Hollis tried to slow her pace. Neither man slackened theirs.

"Sergeant Hollis don't walk any slower. If we have to drag you along the road and pretend that you're drunk we will. Speed up!"

Hollis sped up slightly. She cursed herself. Why hadn't she rung in and said where she was before leaving the car? She had to think of a way to get away from the Southpools. Both men had a firm grip on her arms. There was nothing that she could do.

Hollis stilled the panic in her voice and said, "Threatening a police officer is a criminal offence. What are you going to do? Do anything to me and you will be looking at a long custodial sentence."

Robert Southpool laughed. He said, "You think we care about that?"

Hollis turned and looked at him. Robert Southpool wore a vicious expression; his eyes were ice cold and his lips were thin and colourless. Laura could well believe that this was the person who had killed Jennifer Lindsay. Robert dragged her into a walkway between two buildings. He quickened his pace. Hollis had no option other than to speed up. The compact driveway was silent. It was between two office blocks. No-one was following them, and no-one was coming towards them.

They were walking along a drive way that was leading to a parking area at the back of the flats. No-one was going to know where she was. She looked up at the buildings. There were very few windows. Those that were there were covered in frosted panels or blinds. There were a few cars in the open parking bays. Frederick Southpool's was one of them. Robert walked towards the car.

Frederick Southpool said, "No, I have a better idea. Let's take her upstairs."

Chappell raced his car along the road. Seeing Hollis' abandoned car, he screeched to a halt behind it. All three policemen piled out of the vehicle. Chappell tried the driver's door of Hollis' car. It was unlocked. Her handbag was in full view. Breathing in deeply he placed a hand on the side of the car. The implications of Hollis' disappearance sprang immediately to his mind.

"Hudson and Sampson, we need to find her. She didn't leave this area willingly. If she is with the Southpools, she could be in extreme danger."

Hudson asked, "Would they really do anything to her?"

Chappell nodded, "Think about it for a moment. Each of these men has killed someone. They will have no compunction about killing Hollis. The way I see it they have two options. Either way they kill Hollis and then leave her body in their flat or else in the boot of a car. They would be long gone before she was found. Sampson call for back up. We need more people. Now!"

Chappell and Hudson ran along the road as Sampson put in a call to the police station. Since Hollis had not passed them as they had driven up she must have been taken in the opposite direction. It would be difficult to make her out. There were shoppers, officer workers, students and pensioners all taking up the pavement. Chappell and Hudson dodged past them hoping to see a trace of her.

Chappell asked, "Hudson, you were talking to Hollis this morning, what was she wearing the last time you saw her?"

"Sir, I don't remember. I know she was wearing jeans and maybe a dark sweatshirt."

Chappell nodded and they continued running along the road, looking through shop windows and scanning the pavement ahead of them.

Sampson caught up with them, he said "Back-up is on the way."

Chappell, the desperation, sounding in his voice said, "We have to find her." His height was no advantage to him. He could not see through the crowd in front of him.

"There, there she is between those two men. See them?" Chappell pointed to the trio who had just turned into the walkway. The three policemen dashed down the street and into the walkway.

Hollis focused on thinking about how to escape. With one man she might have been able to overpower him but, with two men gripping her arms there was little she could do. She would have to wait for her chance. It came shortly after. The back door to the block of flats needed to be opened by a key. Frederick Southpool let go of her arm so that he could search his pockets for his keys and then select the right one. Robert Southpool pulled her to one side. This was her chance. She turned, kicked Robert in the groin and punched him in the stomach. He grunted and bent over. Frederick Southpool dropped his keys and moved towards her.

Hollis ran back towards the main road. She did not make it. She ran straight into the arms of Dave Sampson. Chappell and Hudson raced past her and tackled the Southpools. It was a short fight. Robert Southpool put his hands up. He was still in pain from Hollis' powerful kick. His father attempted to land a punch on Hudson. It was an ill-judged move. Hudson punched him twice. Once in the stomach and once to a shoulder.. Southpool didn't attempt to dodge. When Hudson's fist connected with his shoulder Frederick Southpool fell straight to the ground.

The wail of police sirens could be heard in the distance. Chappell walked back to Hollis, while Sampson and Hudson handcuffed the Southpools and led them away to the waiting police vehicles.

Chappell looked at Hollis, ensuring that she was not injured. "They didn't hurt you did they?"

"No, sir. Just my pride." Hollis looked embarrassed.

Chappell laughed, "That will heal Laura. It will heal."

Chappell walked into his office, tidied his desk, and threw the coffee receipts and empty coffee cups into his dustbin. He picked up his latest cup of coffee, leant back in his chair and looked at the picture of the Matterhorn. Another mountain climbed; another mountain conquered. He silently toasted the picture and took a deep draught of his drink.

Outside in the incident room, his team tidied their desks and wrote up their reports.

Hollis asked Sampson and Hudson, "but how did you know?"

Hudson replied, "Hollis you know our boss. Detective Chief Inspector Chappell is always in at the kill."

MILDRED PIERCE

The Film
The 1945 American film noir crime-drama, was based on a novel by James M Cain.

The Storyline
The film, which is based in Glendale, California, starts with a murder. Monte Beragon (Zachary Scott), the second husband of Mildred Pierce (Joan Crawford), is shot dead. The police believe the killer is Bert Pierce (Bruce Bennett), her first husband who confesses to the crime. Mildred Pierce says otherwise and reveals her life story to the investigating officers in flashback.

The dominating personality is Mildred Pierce's daughter, Veda, (Ann Blyth), a bratty social climber. Her mother is dedicated to providing her with material possessions. The film focuses on the convoluted relationships between her second husband (Monte Beragon), a Pasadena society playboy, Mildred and Veda.

In the end, the detectives reveal that they have known all along who committed the murder. Mildred Pierce leaves the police station to meet with a further surprise.

The Production
The director was Hungarian born Michael Curtiz whose Hollywood breakthrough came in 1935 with the casting of an unknown Errol Flynn in the swashbuckling action drama, 'Captain Blood' followed by the 1936 film, 'The Charge of the Light Brigade'. He wanted Bette Davis for the role of Mildred Pierce and had a tense relationship with Joan

Crawford throughout the filming. He went on to become one of Hollywood's most prolific directors.

The producer was Jerry Wald who, despite dying at the age of fifty, made a staggering number of films as writer/producer including Key Largo (1948) and Peyton Place (1957). He was a close friend of Joan Greenwood.

The Stars
The film is dominated by Joan Crawford's Oscar winning performance: she became a Hollywood legend and often played the role of the hard-working young woman who would find romance and success. In 1999, the American Film Institute voted her the tenth greatest female star of classic American cinema. At times a controversial figure, she once said: "I never go outside unless I look like Joan Crawford, the movie star. If you want to look like the girl next door, go next door." She died in 1977 aged seventy-two.

Zackary Scott, an American of Greek descent,, played Monte Beragon early in his career (being his fourth film). He made many more but never really achieved genuine fame. He was subject to bouts of depression and died at the age of 51 of a brain tumour.

American Anne Marie Blyth, who played the key role of Veda, has had a rather varied life as a cinema/television actress, a mother of five children, a devout Catholic and an active Republican supporter. She was nominated for an Oscar for her role in 'Mildred Pierce'. She is ninety years old.

The Book
The author, James Mallahan Cain (1.7.1892 –

27.10.1977), was an American journalist and author. He wrote over twenty-five novels, novellas and many screenplays. He is credited with being one of the creators of 'hardboiled fiction' (sometimes called 'roman noir') whose heyday was 1930 - 50s America. It featured detectives dealing with violent crime within a corrupt legal system. It often featured tough, perhaps cynical, attitudes towards emotions triggered by violence. His first novel, 'The Postman Always Rings Twice' was published in 1934 and was followed, two years later, by 'Double Indemnity', both becoming successful films. 'Mildred Pierce' was written in 1941.

THE NOVELLA NOSTALGIA SERIES

This publishing initiative brings together the uniqueness of the novella and various memorable movies from the history of cinema.

The word 'novella' comes from the Italian for 'novel.' It has been interpreted in various ways including 'a long short story' or a 'short novel'. It can be traced back to the early renaissance in Italy and France. Giovanni Boccaccio wrote 'The Decameron' in 1353. This comprises 100 tales of ten people fleeing the black death. It was not until the 18th and 19th centuries that the novella emerged as a literary genre.

In 1941, the Austrian novelist Stefan Zweig wrote 'The Chess Novella' which was later renamed 'The Royal Game'. This was the inspiration for the 1960 film 'Brainwashed'.

Most modern novellas are published by Penguin Modern Classics. The various novella prizes seem to stipulate a word count of between 7,500 and 40,000. A key feature of the novella is its limited punctuation. There are no chapter headings and no breaks apart from spaces where the author needs to show a scene change.

Full details of the Novella Nostalgia series can be found at www.cityfiction.co.uk.